PUFFIN BOOKS

UK | USA | Canada | Ireland | Australia
India | New Zealand | South Africa

Puffin Books is part of the Penguin Random House group of companies whose
addresses can be found at global.penguinrandomhouse.com.

puffinbooks.com

First published 2015
001

Text and illustrations copyright © Mind Candy, 2015
Written by Richard Jenkins, Steve Cleverley, Mark Knowles Lee and Dan Parry

The moral right of the author and illustrator has been asserted

Printed in Slovakia

A CIP catalogue record for this book is available from the British Library

ISBN: 978–0–141–36032–4

WORLD OF WARRIORS™

OFFICIAL GUIDE

PUFFIN

WELCOME TO THE WORLD OF WARRIORS

World of Warriors is an exciting game that puts you at the heart of a ferocious battle between good and evil. Can you unite history's greatest warriors to defeat evil King Boneshaker and save the Wildlands?

CONTENTS

HISTORY OF THE WILDLANDS

PORTALS OF POWER

Thousands of years ago, mysterious portals were built on wellsprings of pure Battle Power throughout the vast Wildlands. The portals were aligned with the four elemental powers of Water, Fire, Earth and Air, and whenever anyone travelled through them, they would be given awesome power. Not only this, the portals allowed instant transportation throughout the Wildlands, and even to different realms and dimensions.

For many years a mighty empire, overseen by four Elemental Lords (one for each element), ruled the Wildlands. These were harmonious years, as the wise Lords used the portals to maintain peace through the realms.

But a brutal entity known as the Darkness entered the Wildlands through one of the portals, wreaking havoc and destruction.

A terrible war raged, but the four Elemental Lords combined their powers to defeat the Darkness. They sentenced it to imprisonment in the Wildforge, deep within Mount Shadowshard.

Even though they were victorious, the long war had weakened the Elemental Lords. The land was ruined and the people had grown suspicious of the ancient portals, and were fearful of a return of dark forces. With heavy hearts, the Lords decided to leave the Wildlands.

As their final act, the Elemental Lords appointed loyal, stoic warriors known as Gatemen to guard the ancient routes of the Wildlands. The Lords then departed through the portals, sealing them shut forever – except for one…

THE TEMPLE OF EPICS

This single portal, known as the Temple of Epics, was a secret gateway to history. It was left open in case the inhabitants of the Wildlands needed to summon warriors, weapons or items from the past. The four Elemental Lords made sure it could only be opened by those who had performed the most valiant deeds or earned the greatest respect from their peers.

Centuries went by and the portal was all but forgotten, until an evil warrior priest from Earth stumbled through the portal and found himself in the Wildlands, infused with great Battle Power. Thanks to a legend stating that Shadowshard 'would one day shatter, but not by the hand of men from the Wildlands', the warrior priest manipulated the superstitious Wildlanders and seized power, proclaiming himself King Boneshaker.

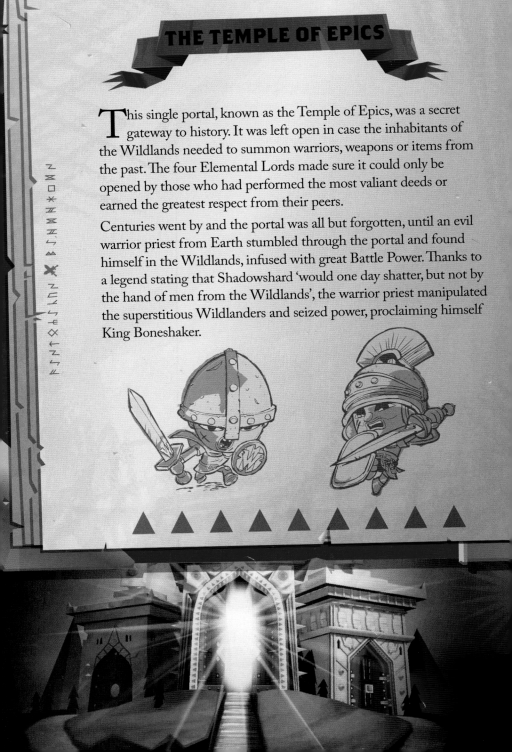

Only one person stood in his way – a brave young man named Kalaban. During one almighty showdown, Boneshaker murdered Kalaban's bride-to-be (a warrior princess from Earth who was dragged through the portal by Boneshaker). Totally distraught, Kalaban attacked Boneshaker. It was a terrible battle that nearly destroyed them both.

A devastated and injured Kalaban fled to the peace of Cloud Lake to meditate and recuperate. Boneshaker crawled to the caves under the soaring peak of Mount Shadowshard, to regain his strength and build a new army.

AND NOW, MANY YEARS LATER…

King Boneshaker has arisen! Corrupted by the Darkness that infects Shadowshard, he has smashed the seals on the Portals and is searching for the power of the Elemental Lords.

His goal? To control this fearsome power and release the Darkness back in the Wildlands. Will you be the one to continue Kalaban's quest and defeat King Boneshaker once and for all? In order to survive this first epic quest, you must battle through fifteen stages of the Wildlands.

THE QUEST

With Kalaban's help you must use the one remaining portal, The Temple of Epics, to summon an army of mighty warriors from history and lead them against King Boneshaker and his Skull Army. Can you fulfil the ancient legend, find the Wildforge and save the Wildlands?

LET BATTLE COMMENCE!

Your quest is to defeat every member of the Skull Army you encounter on your journey through the Wildlands, until you face King Boneshaker himself in the ultimate showdown.

You will amass a powerful army of warriors that will fight with you on your mission. Only history's greatest warriors are summoned to the Wildlands. Don't be surprised if your army contains a Samurai Warrior fighting side by side with a Roman Gladiator.

You will also be aided on your quest by a handful of helpers. Wise old Kalaban, Kaw the crow, and their reluctant allies will appear to offer guidance and advice at different points throughout your journey.

As well as combat and strategy, your worth as a collector and craftsman will be tested. During your time in the Wildlands you will find plenty of goodies to help you. Here are a few items to look out for:

TOP TIP

During battles you'll be able to collect mana and health. Mana allows you to pull off special moves, and health lets you battle for longer. Be sure to avoid the bombs!

GOLD COINS

When you defeat an opponent, you'll collect coins. These can be used to train your warriors to improve their battle stats.

RED WILDSTONES

These are among the rarest of treasures in the whole of the Wildlands and should be spent wisely. Their best use is to unlock the Door of Epics – this is where you'll find the greatest and most valuable warriors.

BLUE HONOUR STONES

Blue gems can be used on the Honour Door for quick unlocks of talismans, potions for a boost in battle and new warriors.

TOP TIP

Red Wildstones can also be used to revive warriors that have died in battle.

MATERIALS

Gold, silver and bronze ingots can be found pretty much everywhere. Other items like Warmelons can only be picked up in certain regions. You'll need these to craft talismans that will help your warriors.

BUILD YOUR ARMY!

Time to gather your army. Eventually you'll have a mighty array of warriors — each with strengths and weaknesses and each with a story to tell. But there's no time for talking when there's fighting to be done!

GATHER YOUR ARMY

To add a warrior to your roster, pay a visit to the Temple of Epics, where warriors from history can be summoned to join forces with you. Once inside, you'll find three doors . . .

TOP TIP

If you summon a warrior that you already own, you can fuse their spirit with the original warrior to give them an XP boost.

WESTERN DOOR

This door is one of the most mysterious places in the whole of the Wildlands. What lies behind it? Venture forth to find out!

RED DOOR – DOOR OF EPICS

This red door costs a whopping ten Wildstones to open, but guarantees you either a Rare (two-star), Super Rare four-star) or Legendary (six-star) warrior.

BLUE DOOR – HONOUR DOOR

This door costs five blue Honour Stones to unlock and is the best place to find talismans, recipes, potions and gold coins. Occasionally a Common (one-star) warrior will pop out. If you're lucky, a rarer warrior might heed your call.

UNDERSTANDING WARRIOR STATS

ELEMENTAL POWER
This shows how much elemental power the warrior has, and also to which element they belong. The higher the number, the greater the damage they can dish out.

UPGRADE LEVEL
This warrior is at level four out of a possible ten. When he reaches 10, it's time to upgrade him in the Home Camp. The warrior's XP bar is low right now but a few battles will fill it up.

PHYSICAL ATTACK
This shows how much damage the warrior is able to inflict with any attack.

SPECIAL MOVE
This tells you what the warrior's special mana-powered move is. The four dots to the right of the icon illustrate the power of the move.

4 10 LANCE The Knight Templar

THUNDER STRIKE
Electrocute enemies with the power of lightning!

★ ★

🗡 28
💧 5
❤ 145
🛡 Heavy

+15% EARTH damage to all of your EARTH warriors

TALISMANS

Heart Token
+5% Max-Health.
6

SKILLS

LOCKED   LOCKED

LOCKED   LOCKED

LOCKED   LOCKED

ARMOUR
This warrior's heavy shield makes him great for defence and able to withstand some mighty blows, but doesn't defend against elemental power.

TALISMANS
This fighter is equipped with a heart talisman, which upgrades his maximum health by 5%. It has six uses left.

HEALTH
This reveals how much of a beating the warrior can take before they get knocked out.

LEADER-SKILL
When your warrior is placed in the Leader position, this shows what boosts he gives the others. Make your most powerful warrior the leader.

SKILLS
Legendary warriors come with two skill slots already unlocked. Upgrade your warrior to unlock more slots and improve your fighting power.

GET COMBAT READY

Here you'll learn the skills necessary to defeat King Boneshaker and his Skull Army. Each warrior has a different attack and it's worth doing some practice now to pull off the most powerful moves later.

TOP TIP

These next moves all use up mana, and are powerful techniques unique to every warrior.

STANDARD BLOW

This is the easiest move to master – simply tap the screen when the sensor reaches the red line of the sword to get a perfect hit. If you don't have any mana, this is your default move.

THREE POINTS

Like the standard blow, but three times trickier! Tap the screen three times as close as possible to the red lines.

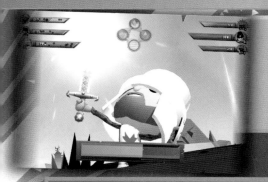

MULTI TAP

For the hardest hits, tap your screen as many times as possible before the timer runs down. If the meter is full by the end, you've scored a perfect hit.

CIRCLE MATCH

A large white circle will appear on screen. Inside, is a smaller red circle. The white circle will shrink down in size until it matches the red one – and when it does, it's time to tap the screen.

NUMBER MATCH

Tap the circles in numerical order as quickly as you can. But watch out; they don't appear in the right order – they're jumbled up.

TOP TIP

The closer your blow is to 'perfect', the more damage it will do to your foe. Practise on weaker enemies for easy wins.

SELECTION WHEEL

Attack any enemy you choose! The sword swings between all your opponents. Whichever opponent you tap on will be targeted and then attacked.

GOING INTO BATTLE

Now that you've mastered the basics of combat, it's time to enter the battlefield and prove your worth as a warrior of valour and strength.

PICK A FIGHT

The only way to survive in the Wildlands is to fight. Some battles will be easier than others, especially early on in the game. Just tap the map icon to start a scrap. You can replay battles as often as you like to build up XP or find loot.

LET BATTLE COMMENCE!

In a battle, you take it in turns with the opposition to trade blows. When you're hit, you can collect mana and health by swiping over the icons that appear on screen while you're dazed. But watch out for bombs!

MANA POWER

This mysterious force lets you unleash powerful attacks. You can see how much you have stored up in the blue meter. Use a mana move by tapping the warrior's icon, or save it for another move and strike a standard blow by tapping the sword icon!

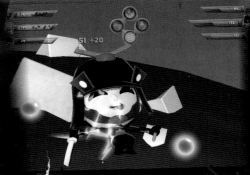

BIG BOSS BATTLES

Looking for trouble? At the end of every one of the Wildlands' fifteen stages, you'll come across a rough, tough boss battle. These are harder than average fights, and will require all of your cunning as a leader, as well as the toughest warriors you've got.

KEEP COLLECTING

One of the best things about winning in battle is the opportunity to hoover up a lot of loot! As you defeat opponents, you can collect coins and crafting materials. (See p26 for info on how to use these.) Coins can be spent in-game on training and upgrading warriors.

TREASURE TIME

Certain battles are made extra special by the presence of a treasure chest, bursting at the seams with goodies! They are ferociously guarded by the Skull Army, but if you win a battle you'll pick up talismans or other treasures.

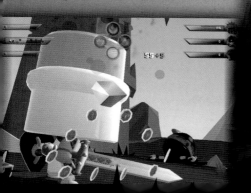

MASTER THE ELEMENTS!

When it comes to battling, the best warriors pay attention to the details. Each warrior and villain in the Wildlands belongs to an elemental class, which gives them awesome abilities. Understanding how these elements work will allow you to inflict serious damage on your enemies.

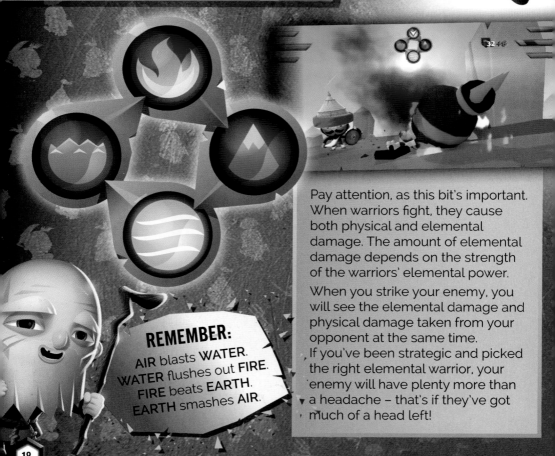

Pay attention, as this bit's important. When warriors fight, they cause both physical and elemental damage. The amount of elemental damage depends on the strength of the warriors' elemental power.

When you strike your enemy, you will see the elemental damage and physical damage taken from your opponent at the same time.
If you've been strategic and picked the right elemental warrior, your enemy will have plenty more than a headache – that's if they've got much of a head left!

REMEMBER:
AIR blasts WATER.
WATER flushes out FIRE.
FIRE beats EARTH.
EARTH smashes AIR.

TOP TIP

If you don't have the warriors you need for maximum elemental destruction then go on the defensive. Pick the warriors that will receive the least elemental pain from your opponents.

BE A POWER PRO

Some warriors have stronger elemental power than others. If you're up against a gang of Fire villains, make sure your warrior team is packed with Water warriors in order to win.

👑 LEADER SKILL:
+15% FIRE damage given to all of your FIRE warriors

ELEMENTAL LEADER-SKILLS

Some warriors have leader-skills that increase the power of elements for your entire team, put them in the leader position and team them up with other warriors of matching element for a big boost in battle.

PORTAL AND TOWER GUIDE

The Portal is a mysterious location that you can visit to fight different battles. It's also a great place to stock up on loot. Each day there are different battles to face, and while winning them won't advance you in the game, they're definitely worth spending time on.

FIND YOUR WAY IN!

You won't be able to enter the Portal until you've beaten RamRaider, the Skull Army Boss that guards Greendeep Valley VIII. When you do, you'll be able to enter the Portal area that appears in the "TO BATTLE" screen.

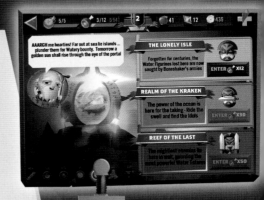

DAILY DELIGHTS

Each day delivers a new battle as well as an essential material for killer crafting:

Mondays – Talisman recipes
Tuesdays – Fire materials
Wednesdays – Earth materials
Thursdays – Air materials
Fridays – Water materials

TOP TIP

Enter the Portal on a Sunday and you'll also be able to earn XP potions for your warriors, to upgrade them faster!

TOP TIP

Tower trophies can only be collected from the top floor – so you'll have to work your way up to get hold of them! However, the rarest materials are won in Tower Leagues.

THE TOWER OF TRIALS

Just above the Portal is the Tower of Trials. Inside here you can fight your way up, floor by floor, to the very top to reap awesome rewards.

DICING WITH DANGER

The Tower of Trials is controlled by Dice and is overflowing with Skull Army minions. It's your job to try and beat them before they rip you to shreds. No easy task! Succeed and you will be able to win materials such as tower tokens and loot, which will improve your chances in battle.

HIGH PRICE

You can only enter the Tower of Trials for free once a day. You have to pay Wildstones and Honour Stones if you want to return again on the same day so make sure you have enough gems banked to do so. There are five floors to make your way through, so stock up on potions and talismans too.

TRAINING YOUR WARRIORS

Your warriors may be strong enough to withstand Boneshaker's menacing Skull Army in the early stages of the game, but it won't be long before they'll need to toughen up.

EARN XP

Every time you use a warrior in battle, they'll gain XP. You can see a warrior's XP rise at the end of every fight.

VISIT HOME CAMP

When your fighters are ready to train, you'll see a flash along the bottom of their card. It's time to visit the Home Camp to get training!

GET TO WORK

Move your warrior up into the training slot, and they'll start pumping iron. The higher the level, the longer this will take. While the warriors are training, you will be unable to use them in battle.

SPEED THINGS UP

You can speed up the training process – for a Wildstone price, but it's probably best to wait, and save your stones.

TOP TIP

It's worth spending ten Wildstones to unlock the second training area. This lets you have two warriors training at once.

COUNT THE COST

Don't forget to keep an eye on your coins – it costs to upgrade the warriors. The higher their level, the higher the price.

UPGRADE

At the top left of a warrior's card you'll see two numbers. These are what level the warrior currently holds, and the highest number it's possible for the warrior to attain. When the two numbers match, it's time to upgrade. This unlocks extra power, as well as new costumes and talisman slots.

THE WAIT IS OVER

After the training period has passed, it's time to summon your warrior back from the Home Camp and let them loose with their upgraded powers.

TALISMAN TIPS

Talismans are key to winning battles. If employed correctly, they can boost your health and inflict major damage on your opponents' stats.

TALISMAN	EFFECT
Air Trinket	Reduces Air damage received.
Fire Trinket	Reduces Fire damage received.
Water Trinket	Reduces Water damage received.
Earth Trinket	Reduces Earth damage received.
Air Medallion	Reduces Air damage received.
Fire Medallion	Reduces Fire damage received.
Water Medallion	Reduces Water damage received.
Earth Medallion	Reduces Earth damage received.
Berserker Token	Reduces max-health and increases total attack.
Berserker Charm	Reduces max-health and increases total attack.
Phoenix Token	Reduces max-health and increases total attack.
Phoenix Trinket	Reduces max-health and increases total attack.
Phoenix Charm	Reduces max-health and increases total attack.
Phoenix Medallion	Reduces max-health and increases total attack.
Phoenix Amulet	Reduces max-health and increases total attack.
Armour Boost	Increases armour level by one.
Coin Multiplier	Collect 20% extra gold from a KO.
Heart Token	Increases max-health.
Heart Trinket	Increases max-health.
Heart Charm	Increases max-health.
Heart Medallion	Increases max-health.
Heart Amulet	Increases max-health.
Heart Magnet	Increases max-health.

TALISMAN	EFFECT
Power Token	Increases total attack.
Power Trinket	Increases total attack.
Power Charm	Increases total attack.
Power Medallion	Increases total attack.
Power Amulet	Increases total attack.
Protection Token	Reduces total attack, increases max-health.
Protection Charm	Reduces total attack, increases max-health.
Mirror Trinket	% damage received is reflected back on their opponent.
Mirror Amulet	% damage received is reflected back on their opponent.
Regeneration Charm	Awards player with small amount of health at the start of each turn.
Regeneration Amulet	Awards player with small amount of health at the start of each turn.
Resilience Charm	Gain health back during health heart collection.
Resilience Medallion	Gain 50% health back during health heart collection.
Poison Amulet	All poison effects last one extra turn.
Assassin Token	Gives a random warrior on your team extra health after a KO.
Assassin Charm	Gives a random warrior on your team extra health after a KO.
Assassin Amulet	Gives a random warrior on your team extra health after a KO.
Justice Trinket	Poisons your attacker if one of your warriors is knocked out.
Justice Charm	Poisons your attacker if one of your warriors is knocked out.
Justice Amulet	Poisons your attacker if one of your warriors is knocked out.
Crossfire Charm	Allows regular attacks to strike all members of the opposing team.
Crossfire Medallion	Allows regular attacks to strike all members of the opposing team.
Crossfire Amulet	Allows regular attacks to strike all members of the opposing team.
Revenge Trinket	Increases your warrior's power when they are the last member of your team standing.
Revenge Medallion	Increases your warrior's power when they are the last member of your team standing.
Mana Steal	Regular attacks radomly steal mana from the enemy.
Break Trinket	Slowly reduces the strength of your opponent's weapon when you are attacked.
Break Medallion	Slowly reduces the strength of your opponent's weapon when you are attacked.
Promotion	Allows any warrior to use their leader-skill even when they are not selected as the leader of a team.

CRAFTING GUIDE

It is within your power to forge epic boosts for your battles. Now it's time to learn what materials you need to create them in the Foundry.

GOT IT

GOT IT

- Silver Ingot
- Emblem of Glory
- Air Figurine
- Bronze Ingot
- Fire Totem
- Tower Token
- Gold Ingot
- Purewater
- Water Idol
- Water Totem
- Almnut
- Air Idol
- Air Totem

- Tower Trophy
- Fire Idol
- Warmelon
- Fire Figurine
- Water Figurine
- Earth Idol
- Earth Figurine
- Earth Totem
- Mistwood
- Toadthrone
- Skull Rune
- Etherwine

26

There are dozens of different charms, boosts and trinkets to make, each with different benefits in battle. As soon as you've got the right materials (and discovered the scroll with the recipe), just hit CRAFT and the Foundry will do the rest.

Here are a few recipes to get your mouth watering . . .

Mirror Trinket
Boost: Reflects 7% of all incoming damage

Needed: 2x Bronze Ingot
5x Honour Stones
Gold Coins

Resilience Token
Boost: Extra 5% health in heart collection

Needed: 3x Silver Ingot
2x Gold Ingot
2x Tower Token
Gold Coins

Berserker Charm
Boost: +35% attack, -25% health

Needed: 1x Fire Figurine
3x Gold Ingot
1x Tower Token
Gold Coins

TOP TIP

To see how much stuff you're holding, just head to the Foundry and click the inventory button. Once you're done crafting, you can equip your warriors.

THE ALLIES

The quest that faces you is not an easy one. It will be fraught with danger and death, but you will not face this battle alone. On your journey through the vast Wildlands you will meet many allies, who will appear throughout the game to give you information that will aid your progress. Be warned though, some will be more helpful to you than others...

A B C D E F G H I J K L M N O P Q R S T U V W X Y Z

_____ __ _____ __ _____

____ ____. ___ ____ ___ ____ _____

___ ___ __ ____ _____ ___ _____ __

_____ ____ _____ ___ ___ _____

____ __ ____ ___ _____ ____ ____!

KALABAN

Don't be fooled by his creaky demeanor. Kalaban was once a fierce Wildlands warrior who battled valiantly against the forces of evil until a massive battle with King Boneshaker forced him into hiding for many years. Today, still wanted by the Skull Army for his role in the Elemental Uprising, this honourable leader acts as a mentor to summoned warriors, and can always be relied upon to offer wisdom, guidance and the occasional Wildstone!

LIKES: The greatest warriors in history.

DISLIKES: Mesopotamian priests.

KAW THE MESSENGER

Scouring the Wildlands for signs of danger, Kaw is the feathery friend who Kalaban has come to rely upon as his trusted aerial scout. Jumpy and jittery due to the dreadful things he witnessed while forced to work as a messenger crow for the Skull Army, Kaw is keen to make amends, so he now flies over danger zones in the hope that he can save lives and maybe even pick up a few tasty worms along the way.

LIKES: Gleaming treasure.

DISLIKES: Flaming arrows.

KIRK STONEBACK

A great warrior and former undefeated champion of the Arenas of TempestGuard, Kirk was forced to retire after rearranging a corrupt referee's face with his fists. These days he uses his vast experience to whip zeroes into heroes in his legendary Training Camp. But victory costs, and this bad-tempered trainer makes would-be winners pay in blood, sweat and Wildstones. If Kirk can't turn you into a winner, no one can!

LIKES: Grit and determination.
DISLIKES: Wimps.

ORLANDER

Former potion trader, used cart salesman and hustler of huge repute, Orlander is now the greatest fight promoter in the Wildlands. Well that's what he tells everyone. The truth is . . . well, no one really knows the truth because Orlander's stories are almost as tall as the Tower of Trials over which he once presided. When he isn't busy dreaming up new money making schemes, this kind-hearted rascal enjoys drinking vintage mead with his former pirate crewmates and overseeing the Wildlands' ever-expanding array of awesome Arenas.

LIKES: Offshore tax avoidance schemes.
DISLIKES: Too many questions.

BELTHRAX THE SORCERESS

Although this mysterious sorceress insists upon speaking in rhymes, her knowledge of ancient lore, elemental powers and lost languages remains unrivalled. Feared by superstitious strangers but respected by close friends such as Kalaban and Kirk, Belthrax can be unreliable and often vanishes without warning. Some say she disappears to study her Ancient Scrolls of Lore, others fear she is busy practising dark magic. Kalaban, on the other hand, believes she meets with her sorceress sisters, many of whom remain wanted by the Skull Army.

LIKES: Translating ancient runes.
DISLIKES: Straight talk.

GATEKEEPER

Are there several Gatemen or just one? Nobody knows for sure because this mysterious cloaked character crops up all over the Wildlands. Some say he is the lone survivor of an ancient brotherhood of powerful guardians, others believe he simply enjoys flitting from gate to gate, hampering warriors' progress. Whatever the Gatekeeper's motivation might be, if he doesn't like the look of you, you're not getting through.

LIKES: Hindering gatecrashers.
DISLIKES: Trainers (especially Kirk).

WHITE WASTES

DOSVIROE GLACIER

BITTERFROST FALL

EN FINGERS

SHADOWSHARD

THE ICE GUARDIANS

STORMCLOUD STAIR

BLACKSKULL PASS

RAVEN RAVINE

LOCH OF THE LONGICE

S SPLINTERS

TALLMAN'S FOLLY

THE SKULL GATE

OLD GHOUL TOWER

SKULL CITY

DARK SILVER MINES

PLAINS OF KALSEA

SKULL PASS

KHANKILL NOBBLES

HOLLOW HACKMAN

MOUNT MARKITZURO

SULPURNIUS

LACK UNTLET

VOLCANO CANYON

DOMES OF ALKAZAR

RITHALIM'S BASTION

REDROCK RING

FIREDUST FLIGHTHEN

SANDALUS DESERT

THE GOLDEN OCEAN

TEI LOST PEAK

THE SHIFTING GROUND

THE LOST STONES

F SANDALUS

WANDERING SANDS

BLACKWAVE BAY

PLAIN OF SWORDS

MAP OF THE

WILDLANDS

SHADOW LANDS

WARRIORS LANDING

WARRIORS LANDING I

This is a real beginner's test – surely you can take down just one foe? Remember everything you've learned in your training to beat them.

WARRIORS LANDING II

Double trouble! Can you beat two enemies? You will need to head to the Temple to unlock another warrior if one's not enough.

WARRIORS LANDING III

Another pair from the Skull Army! These guys don't even have elemental power, so you should be able to take them down using brute force.

WARRIORS LANDING IV

Now it's getting serious. Three enemies this time, although they still won't give you any elemental trouble.

WARRIORS LANDING V

Now you're up against elemental power – luckily you can bring in three warriors of your own. Make sure to check which elements work best against these opponents.

WARRIORS LANDING VI

You're nearly at the end of your first test. Which elements would be best for tackling these brutes?

WARRIORS LANDING VII

These Skull Army warriors are all level two, which means they'll be able to take and deliver more damage – you won't have fought anyone this tough yet. So get ready!

GREENDEEP VALLEY

GREENDEEP VALLEY I

Just two enemies to knock out here. Piece of cake! The enemies will only be using standard blows, so you should be able to take care of them easily enough.

GREENDEEP VALLEY II

Things have just got trickier! Three enemies to fight and each has been levelled up to two. The higher the enemy's level is, the harder they'll hit.

GREENDEEP VALLEY III

Only two of these enemies have special moves, so keep an eye on their mana meter. Try and take them down before they can fill it up.

WARRIOR WISDOM

In South Africa, Xhosa warriors carried six assegai (spears) into battle. They would throw the first five, then break the handle off the sixth and use it as a long knife in hand-to-hand combat.

GREENDEEP VALLEY IV

Two pieces of meat per battle might not seem a lot now, but it'll add up and you'll need to wait for more to battle on.

TOP TIP

As well as the story battles, there are random encounters to be found on every map. Take them on for increased XP and loot!

WARRIOR WISDOM

Between 883 and 859 BC, human skins were stuck on city walls in Turkey and Syria by invading Assyrian warriors who had flayed (skinned) the rebel commanders alive.

GREENDEEP VALLEY V *PUZZLE FIGHT – Elemental Teams*

In an Elemental Teams Puzzle Fight you'll face off against an enemy team of just one element. This means your warrior roster is really important. You'll need plenty of warriors against these enemies.

GREENDEEP VALLEY VI

The Skull Army fighters you'll face off against now are level three and up. It's time to get serious.

GREENDEEP VALLEY VII

Beware MadKat's Berserker move. It'll drain your health quicker than you can call for Kalaban's help. And don't forget to bring in some damage healers as well or you'll have a tough time with Fester and Raze.

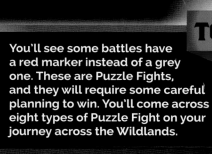

TOP TIP

You'll see some battles have a red marker instead of a grey one. These are Puzzle Fights, and they will require some careful planning to win. You'll come across eight types of Puzzle Fight on your journey across the Wildlands.

BOSS FIGHT

GREENDEEP VALLEY VIII

The terrifying Skull Boss RamRaider awaits. His Phantom Strike move will inflict serious damage on your whole squad.

PHANTOM STRIKE

TOP TIP

Talisman recipes are regularly found in loot chests.

MATERIALS TO FIND:

 Bronze Ingot

 Silver Ingot

 Gold Ingot

BONEHENGE

BONEHENGE I

Your first test in the new land is against some level four warriors. Don't forget: the enemy is just as smart as you when it comes to using elemental advantages.

WARRIOR WISDOM

More than 4,000 years ago, the rulers of the ancient city Akkad in Mesopotamia (today part of the Middle East) built one of the first empires in history by combining archers, spearmen and chariots in one army – an idea that was new at the time.

BONEHENGE II

A nasty lot led by a Water enemy await you here. Don't forget to equip with any talismans or trinkets you've got stored in your inventory.

BONEHENGE III

The mysterious leader of this brute squad has the power to heal his teammates. If you take him down first, the others won't be far behind.

BONEHENGE IV

Running low on meat? Either wait for it to regenerate or spend a few stones to refill.

BONEHENGE V

The leader of these Skull Army warriors is Gobber, who is a fearsome foe, but susceptible to elemental damage just like anyone else.

BONEHENGE VI

Another step up – these enemies are level five.
Can you keep up? Try equipping your warriors
with some talismans to give them a boost.

BONEHENGE VII

Two Air warriors await – go heavy with your Earth
warriors for an elemental advantage, and watch
their HP (health points) disappear.

BONEHENGE VIII

Only two enemies here, but they're both level five, and they're both tough as nails. Make sure your warriors are trained up to match them.

TOP TIP

Some map locations are guarded with a padlock – you'll need to pass certain tests to be able to get through.

BONEHENGE IX

These three will certainly pose a challenge. Head to the Temple to get more warriors if you find the ones you have aren't tough enough.

BOSS FIGHT

BONEHENGE X

Uh-oh . . . Keelok is wearing a Mega Armour talisman! A strong physical attack will hardly scratch him. Go in for the kill with a warrior that has a high elemental attack and Water alignment.

PUZZLE FIGHT –
Mega Armour

BONEHENGE X

COST: 5

LOOT: 12

ACCEPT

MATERIALS TO FIND:

 Bronze Ingot

 Silver Ingot

 Gold Ingot

 Warmelons

 Purewater

DRAGONHILL FORT

DRAGONHILL FORT I

There are only two enemies to take down here, but they're a tough level six so be careful. Dragonhill Fort is a real step up so make sure you're battle-ready.

DRAGONHILL FORT II

The cost of fighting has gone up to five meats – pricey, but with high reward.

DRAGONHILL FORT III   *PUZZLE FIGHT – Bomb*

Only one enemy? This'll be easy . . . won't it? Don't get complacent. If you let Dungo store up enough mana, he'll use his special move and you'll lose instantly. Defeat him by equipping your team with the right talismans and picking your best damage dealers.

WARRIOR WISDOM

Mexico's Aztec kings didn't have permanent armies, but instead relied on armed citizens led by professional soldiers – like the elite Eagle warriors, whose bladed weapons were made of obsidian (volcanic glass that's sharper than steel).

DRAGONHILL FORT IV

It's back up to three enemies now. Earth and Fire warriors will give you a better chance. Try some characters whose mana attacks will damage all your opponents at once.

DRAGONHILL FORT V

Keep an eye on the enemy's mana meter and make sure get in before Flak releases his ferocious Firestorm move!

DRAGONHILL FORT VI   *PUZZLE FIGHT – Mega Armour*

Who is that masked member of the Skull Army? It's hard to tell, but they're wearing Mega Armour. Try using poison to lower the enemy's XP, as regular blows just won't do it.

DRAGONHILL FORT VII

Three warriors, and this time they're all at level seven. Make sure your army matches up by replaying some early battles for an XP boost.

L FORT VIII

...ean the opposition will be regaining a
...e lots of attacks to hurt multiple foes.

WARRIOR WISDOM

The Byzantines flame-grilled their enemies using
pumps that sprayed 'Greek fire', which was hard to
put out. It was made from secret ingredients, and
the recipe is still a mystery!

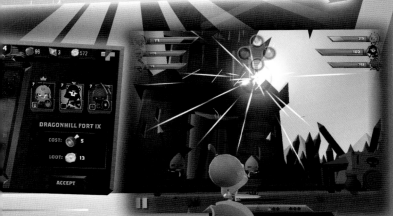

L FORT IX

...h – a mix of warriors is
...e you equipping your warriors
...ismans for maximum effect?

BOSS FIGHT

DRAGONHILL FORT X

It's time to do battle with BoarHammer, and he won't stop until one of you is dead! Level eight, Mega Armour – load up with Fire and poison warriors, and do your best.

BERSERKER

TOP TIP

If you find you're short of materials, go back through the different stages. Each one will offer various goodies to collect.

MATERIALS TO FIND:

  Bronze Ingot

 Silver Ingot

 Gold Ingot

 Warmelons

 Purewater

FIRE WARRIORS

The Fire warriors all have one thing in common: the ability to really put the burn on their opposition. From the lowest levels up to the Legendary fighters, these guys are all fearsome additions to your army. Their elemental power is strongest against Earth warriors.

COMMON

ABU *THE MAMLUK WARRIOR SLAVE*

YEAR: 1302 AD   **WEAPON:** Scimitar

BIO: Having repelled both the Mongols and the Crusaders, Abu was settling down to life as the sultan's chief assassin when he was summoned to the Wildlands.

SPECIAL MOVE: His **Inferno** move burns enemies to a crisp, and when he's placed in the Leader position he gives your other Fire warriors a 15% boost in elemental damage. Abu's only weakness is that he just doesn't hit very hard.

ELEMENTAL POWER: 15   **ARMOUR:** Medium

COMMON

BRUTUS *THE ROMAN SOLDIER*

YEAR: 79 AD   **WEAPON:** Gladius

BIO: Formerly stationed in Pompeii, Brutus was transported to the Wildlands while attempting to control a riot triggered by an escaped tiger in the amphitheatre.

SPECIAL MOVE: He rocks heavy armour and has a cool **Soul Steal** move that nicks health from his enemies and restores his own. In the early parts of the game, he's a good all-rounder to suck up a lot of enemy damage.

ELEMENTAL POWER: 4   **ARMOUR:** Heavy

NARO
THE SIAMESE WARRIOR

YEAR: 1584 AD   **WEAPON:** Dha

BIO: After years of devoted service, Naro's loyalty crumbled when he was overlooked for promotion. He led a brutal rebellion against his kingdom before the Wildlands called him.

SPECIAL MOVE: Naro's **Thunder Strike** takes all of his frustrations out on his foes. He also provides a 25% increase in physical attack to teammates when he's leader.

ELEMENTAL POWER: 13

ARMOUR: Medium

IVAN *THE RUS BOGATYR*

YEAR: 981 AD   **WEAPON:** Sword

BIO: Hairy Ivan vowed not to shave until he'd bumped off at least fifty Tatar invaders. Just as he raised his sword to attack, this rowdy warrior was summoned to the Wildlands, beard and all!

SPECIAL MOVE: His **Phantom Strike** inflicts high physical damage on all of his enemies. If there were any Tatar invaders to use it on, he'd be shaving in no time.

ELEMENTAL POWER: 4

ARMOUR: Medium

YING *THE SONG DYNASTY WARRIOR*

YEAR: 971 AD   **WEAPON:** Dao War Sword

BIO: Battling the mighty war elephant corps of the Southern Han army, Ying was reloading his crossbow when he got distracted by thoughts of his youngest son and closed his eyes. When he opened them, he was in the Wildlands.

SPECIAL MOVE: Ying parries opponents' ordinary strikes with the sneaky **Counter Blow** attack. It saves his skin while turning the enemy's own energy against them.

ELEMENTAL POWER: 15

ARMOUR: Heavy

WARRIOR WISDOM

The earliest true recipe for gunpowder was written in China around 1040 during the Song Dynasty, when it was used in flamethrowers against Mongol armies to the north.

SUPER RARE

BOUDICA *THE ICENI WARRIOR QUEEN*

YEAR: 60 AD   **WEAPON:** Long Sword

BIO: Summoned as she tore through the entire Roman 9th Legion aboard her scythed chariot, Boudica finds life in the Wildlands frustrating because she misses leading her Iceni clan.

SPECIAL MOVE: She cheers herself up by practising her awesome **Switch Strike** move. In a fight, her Critical Hit skill means she will sometimes land a killer blow. She's also got a high level of HP, which means she'll outlast most other warriors.

ELEMENTAL POWER: 10

ARMOUR: Medium

PELION *THE SPARTAN WARRIOR*

YEAR: 480 BC   **WEAPON:** Kopis

BIO: Surrounded by Persian invaders, Pelion was fighting alongside King Leonidas when he suddenly remembered a strange prediction. Before he could warn his king, he was summoned to the Wildlands.

SPECIAL MOVE: Pelion's **Bombard** is an extremely nifty long-range attack that calls a delayed Air strike on his opponents. It's perfect for turning the tables on a tough foe.

ELEMENTAL POWER: 19   **ARMOUR:** Light

SUPER RARE

ISAK *THE NUBIAN HUNTER*

YEAR: 300 BC   **WEAPON:** Shotel Sword

BIO: Lurking behind a sand dune above the Nile, Isak was preparing to sneak aboard a Roman barge when he was whisked to the mysterious Wildlands.

SPECIAL MOVE: Isak drains all the opposition team's health with his **Poison Hive** – so it's best utilized when up against larger groups. Isak's an elemental hero, too, giving other Fire warriors a 30% boost.

ELEMENTAL POWER: 15

ARMOUR: Light

ZUMA *THE JAGUAR WARRIOR*

YEAR: 1519 AD   **WEAPON:** Macuahuitl

BIO: Before entering the Wildlands, Zuma enraged fellow Jaguar soldiers with his reckless use of poison arrows – but you'll find them extremely useful if you recruit him into your army.

SPECIAL MOVE: He's got skills coming out of his jaguar ears. His **Poison move drains his opponent's energy slowly as battle rages on.**

ELEMENTAL POWER: 92

ARMOUR: Light

HUNERIC *THE VANDAL KING*

YEAR: 484 AD   **WEAPON:** Long Seax

BIO: Summoned as he prepared to smash a jagged rock over the head of yet another pretender to his throne, Huneric wanders the Wildlands searching for his beloved wife.

SPECIAL MOVE: It's a surprise – literally. Huneric's speciality is that he will randomly pull off an incredible move belonging to another warrior. He's also packing poison **Antidote** and a Shell which increases his armour.

ELEMENTAL POWER: 87   **ARMOUR:** Heavy

WARRIOR WISDOM

After the Vandals – a tribe originally from central Europe – attacked Rome, their prisoners were sold as slaves, their artworks were stolen and others were damaged, leading to a new word: vandalism.

DAO *THE TRAN DYNASTY WARRIOR*

YEAR: 1284 AD   **WEAPON:** Dha

BIO: Retreating from Mongol invaders led by the mighty Kublai Khan, Dao was scorching villages and crops when he tried to leap aboard an abandoned riverboat. He was summoned to the Wildlands before he hit the deck.

SPECIAL MOVE: **Team Strike** is not to be used lightly – it draws health from your whole team to use against enemies. Dao also has great skills like Hunter, which boosts elemental power against weakly aligned opponents.

ELEMENTAL POWER: 48   **ARMOUR:** Heavy

VLAD *THE WALLACHIAN COUNT*

YEAR: 1477 AD   **WEAPON:** Sabre

BIO: Having just impaled his sixteenth victim of the day, Vlad followed a bat into a cave, eager to skewer something different. He dashed into the darkness brandishing his sword, but felt a blinding surge of energy and found himself in the Wildlands.

SPECIAL MOVE: His special move is **Soul Steal,** which attacks enemies while restoring his own health. Having him as Leader means your team receives 30% less Fire damage – ideal for Elemental Teams.

ELEMENTAL POWER: 34

ARMOUR: Medium

MOONLIGHT MEADOW

MOONLIGHT MEADOW I

A lethal welcome to the Moonlight Meadow awaits you as Ded-Fang and SirPent stand guard. Load up with Water and Earth warriors to beat them.

MOONLIGHT MEADOW II

Three foes, each at level eight. Dark-Dirk has the power to restore his teammates' health, so use Switch Strike blows to take him out early.

TOP TIP

Found a route you can't go down yet? Make a note of it and come back when you're qualified – there will be rare loot to find.

MOONLIGHT MEADOW III

PUZZLE FIGHT – ELEMENTAL IMMUNITY

This sort of Puzzle Fight works in the opposite way to Mega Armour. Your opponents will take almost no elemental damage, so use heavy-hitters to win.

WARRIOR WISDOM

To prepare themselves for a battle, Viking warriors called 'berserkers' would dress in the skin of a bear and work themselves into a trance-like fury, either by willpower or through drugged food.

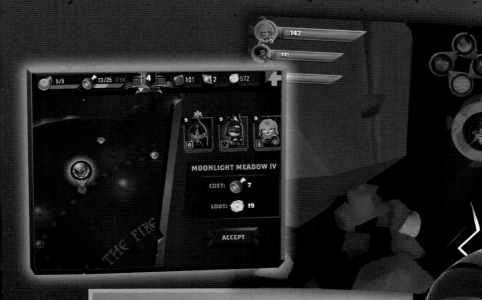

MOONLIGHT MEADOW IV

Three enemies here, each a tough level nine. Once again, do your best to nullify Dark-Dirk 's power to give his teammates a health boost.

WARRIOR WISDOM

When Mayan warriors weren't beheading their enemies or hitting them using clubs spiked with volcanic glass (obsidian), they liked to drip blood from their own tongues to show respect to their gods.

MOONLIGHT MEADOW V

Just two enemies to dispatch here. A powerful Air warrior, an Earth one and a health-boosting character for luck will get you through.

MOONLIGHT MEADOW VI *PUZZLE FIGHT – Fully Loaded*

Your enemy starts with full mana and has a devastating attack. The only way to survive his initial onslaught is to load up with warriors that have high HP, or are equipped with damage-reduction or health talismans.

MOONLIGHT MEADOW VII

Three enemies, each at level ten. If you have any warriors that need training, take them off and get them levelled up now – you'll need all your warriors as tough as possible.

WARRIOR WISDOM

Armed with swords, spears and bows, and protected by leather armour decorated with gold leaf, Tibetan warriors pushed into China and India under emperors like Khri-lde-gtsug-brtsan, better known as 'Old Hairy'.

TOP TIP

Taking part in easier battles will allow you to gather more materials. If you are feeling under-resourced in later fights, track back and stock up on ingots and other materials before tackling harder fights.

BOSS FIGHT

MOONLIGHT MEADOW VIII

Obsidiux, Harbinger of Darkness, is the leader of this band of level eleven enemies. He's tough enough to cause you some serious trouble, and his Elemental Shift special move means you can never tell how he's going to attack.

MATERIALS TO FIND:

 Bronze Ingot   Silver Ingot   Gold Ingot   Warmelons   Purewater

DARKFORT DEEP

DARKFORT DEEP I

These two members of the Skull Army are both a formidable level eleven. Wurmslime's Soul Steal move will drain your health while filling his own.

DARKFORT DEEP II

Three enemies this time – is your squad deep enough to handle all of them? Look out for Niteskull, who'll suck away your mana.

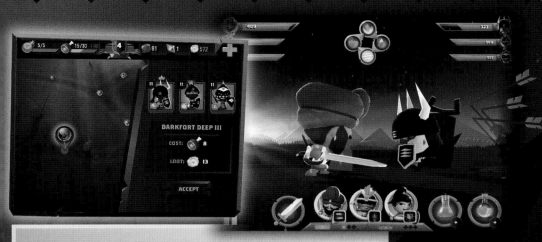

DARKFORT DEEP III *PUZZLE FIGHT – Elemental Teams*

Remember, in one of these fights all of the opposition are of the same element – in this case, it's Air warriors. Anti-Air boosters are a must here, as are plenty of Earth warriors.

TOP TIP

When your warriors get stuck behind their level caps, you have to upgrade them to a higher star rating. Try your luck at the Temple of Epics to find warriors with higher stars.

DARKFORT DEEP IV

Just two enemies in this battle. However, both of them have the power to whittle away your health with their special moves. Keep reinforcements on hand.

DARKFORT DEEP V

Conjunctus's Mimic attack allows him to randomly pull off a special move belonging to one of your own warriors. Don't use any that are too powerful, or you could end up seeing them used against you.

DARKFORT DEEP VI *PUZZLE FIGHT – Toxic*

While the lead enemy is alive, all of your heroes are poisoned! Take him down quickly by using attacks like Switch Strike, which can bring him back into combat if he tries to switch out.

TOP TIP

Picked up some talismans you don't need? You can sell them in the Foundry and put the proceeds towards something even better!

DARKFORT DEEP VII

Two ghoulish Earth warriors and a Water warrior round off the latest batch of Boneshaker's henchmen. Send in the Fire warriors to burn these bad guys up.

DARKFORT DEEP VIII

MadKat's Berserker attack will seriously deplete your warriors' health. Make him your priority, and the other two enemies will fall easily.

DARKFORT DEEP IX *PUZZLE FIGHT – Meatshield*

Behind the tough guy in the ring lies your true enemy: the Stealth Striker. He can jump in and cause lots of damage without you being able to lay a finger on him. Use Switch Strike or multi-foe attacks to wear him down.

DARKFORT DEEP X

Ten battles in and there are still more to come. Darkfort Deep is as much about stamina as it is strength. Take some time to regenerate some meat.

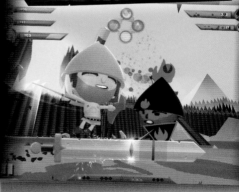

DARKFORT DEEP XI

Just two foes to fight, but be careful with your elemental choices. While Water is strong against Flak's Fire, it's weak against Gruft's Air.

BOSS FIGHT

DARKFORT DEEP XII

Kalaban has some wise words for you ahead of this showdown with the Skull Boss Obsidiux. Your opponent is also rocking Mega Armour, so bring out the poison.

MATERIALS TO FIND:

Bronze Ingot

Silver Ingot

Gold Ingot

Warmelons

Almnuts

SHEERFALL CHASM

SHEERFALL CHASM I

Now you're on the trail of the mysterious Citadel. Belthrax believes it is the last known location of the legendary Wildforge. But watch out! Skull Army forces are everywhere . . .

SHEERFALL CHASM II

It's going to cost you ten meat to fight each of these battles. If you're in a rush, spend gems to refill your stamina.

SHEERFALL CHASM III

These two may be trickier than they look. Slimius's Resurrection move has the power to bring your fallen foe back to life after you've knocked him out.

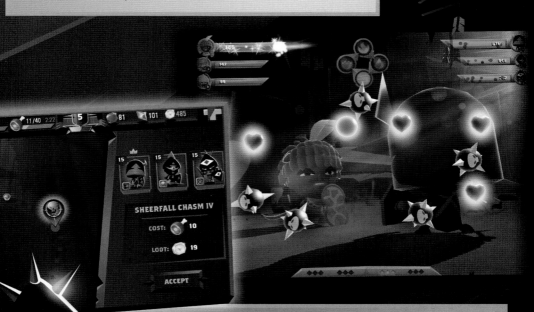

SHEERFALL CHASM IV *PUZZLE FIGHT – Elemental Teams*

Not only are these three brutes tougher than any you've faced, they are all also Earth warriors. A few Fire warriors will send them packing. Not got any? Visit the Temple to summon more.

SHEERFALL CHASM V

Three level fifteen enemies to take down here, from a variety of elements – plus Conjunctus's special move is Mimic, which lets him copy one of your special moves. Take in lots of armour.

SHEERFALL CHASM VI

Lots of Water warriors here, so load up with two Air and one Earth to take out that pesky Gruft in the middle of the pack.

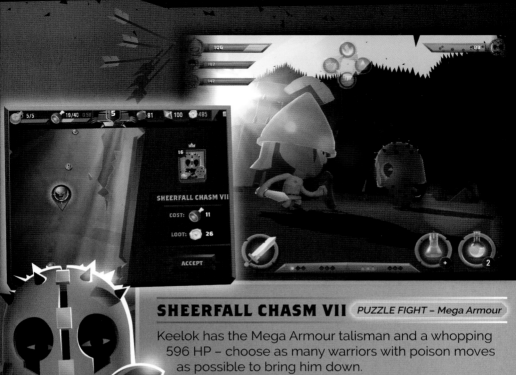

SHEERFALL CHASM VII   *PUZZLE FIGHT – Mega Armour*

Keelok has the Mega Armour talisman and a whopping 596 HP – choose as many warriors with poison moves as possible to bring him down.

SHEERFALL CHASM VIII

It'll cost you eleven meats to take on these three Skull Army warriors. They're a mix of elements, so try to damage the entire team with mana moves.

SHEERFALL CHASM IX

Three rock-solid level sixteen enemies guard the gateway to the boss. They're out to drain your health and your mana!

WARRIOR WISDOM

Descended from Vikings, Varangian warriors (from what is now Russia and Ukraine) were known for their legendary fighting ability. Swinging two-handed battleaxes, they fought for the great Byzantine Empire as mercenaries (hired soldiers).

BOSS FIGHT

SHEERFALL CHASM X

Don't let Dungo collect enough mana to power up his Bomb attack or it's good night to your entire team! Bring out big hitters to battle through his light armour as quickly as possible.

SHEERFALL CHASM X

COST: 12

LOOT: 33

17

MATERIALS TO FIND:

Bronze Ingot

Silver Ingot

Gold Ingot

Warmelons

Almnuts

MIDNIGHT FOREST

MIDNIGHT FOREST I

Welcome to the dark and moody Midnight Forest. The enemies in this first battle are all level seventeen. Can your warriors keep up?

TOP TIP

Using a red boost potion increases the effectiveness of your next move – be it healing, attack or a special move.

MIDNIGHT FOREST II

Niteskull's Drain move will suck away your mana, and Mudd's Boulder Bash will harm your entire team. Make no mistake – this is a tricky battle.

MIDNIGHT FOREST III *PUZZLE FIGHT – Elemental Immunity*

Frakus is equipped with an Elemental Shield which protects him from elemental damage – so your Air warriors won't do much good. Stock up on warriors with high physical damage.

WARRIOR WISDOM

In 1288, around 400 Mongol boats were caught on wooden spikes submerged in the waters of Vietnam's Bach Dang river. Troops of the Vietnamese Tran Dynasty then engaged thousands of Mongol invaders in vicious hand-to-hand combat.

MIDNIGHT FOREST IV

There may only be two enemies to defeat here, but they're both level eighteen. They've only got light armour so, once again, heavy hitters are the key to victory.

MIDNIGHT FOREST V

This battle will test your stamina – you'll have your mana sucked away, while being slowly poisoned. Plus, Dark-Dirk will be refilling his teammates' health. Lots of health talismans are needed here.

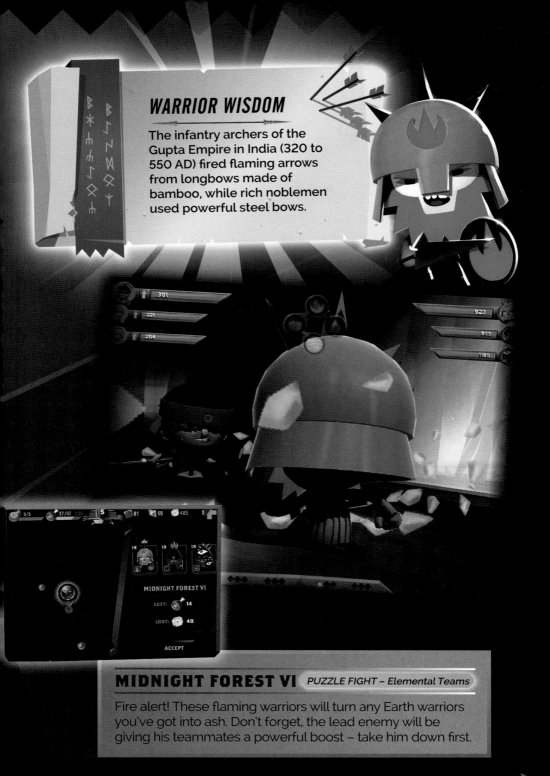

WARRIOR WISDOM

The infantry archers of the Gupta Empire in India (320 to 550 AD) fired flaming arrows from longbows made of bamboo, while rich noblemen used powerful steel bows.

MIDNIGHT FOREST VI

COST: 14

LOOT: 40

ACCEPT

MIDNIGHT FOREST VI *PUZZLE FIGHT – Elemental Teams*

Fire alert! These flaming warriors will turn any Earth warriors you've got into ash. Don't forget, the lead enemy will be giving his teammates a powerful boost – take him down first.

ICE STORM

MIDNIGHT FOREST VII

You're nearly through this section. Do you have enough meat for the battle? If not, take a short break or spend some stones.

WARRIOR WISDOM

Inca warriors used the lethal macana, a star-shaped piece of stone that could be swung on a rope or mounted on a wooden shaft to pulverize heads and bones.

BOSS FIGHT

MIDNIGHT FOREST VIII

It's your first encounter with Slice and Dice. This deadly duo is a formidable combination. Slice is also packing a Saboteur talisman, which means she'll add bombs to your mana and health collection, so take care.

MATERIALS TO FIND:

Bronze Ingot   Silver Ingot   Gold Ingot

Almnuts   Mistwood

WATER WARRIORS

Get ready to drench the opposition with these mighty Water warriors. Brave and brutal, none will let you down in battle. They're super strong against Fire, but vulnerable to attacks from Air — so use them wisely.

ZENGIS
THE MONGOL WARRIOR

YEAR: 1235 AD   **WEAPON:** Sabre

BIO: This sabre-wielding warrior is legendary for leading several brutal campaigns on horseback against the Jin Dynasty. Don't make him angry!

SPECIAL MOVE: His **Frozen Crunch** move freezes his enemies solid. Even handier is his ability as Leader to make his team take 15% less Air damage – a must-have for anyone serious about using elemental power to the maximum.

ELEMENTAL POWER: 19   **ARMOUR:** Medium

RAM *THE EGYPTIAN WARRIOR*

YEAR: 1330 BC   **WEAPON:** Khopesh

BIO: Lost in a fierce sandstorm after falling from his chariot during a skirmish with some Nubians, Ram took shelter in a plundered tomb. He fell asleep, only to wake up in the Wildlands.

SPECIAL MOVE: When Ram is in the Leader position, all Water characters get a 15% elemental-damage boost. His **Poison** arrows will slowly drain the health of the enemy.

ELEMENTAL POWER: 8   **ARMOUR:** Light

YADA
THE FEROCIOUS PHOENICIAN

YEAR: 965 BC   **WEAPON:** Kopis

BIO: Hand-picked to guard a precious cargo en route to Carthage, Yada was below decks honing his sword when he heard screaming. A mutiny was afoot, but Yada was summoned to the Wildlands before he could stop it.

SPECIAL MOVE: Yada uses **Thunder Strike** to electrocute enemies with the power of lightning – provided he's got the mana to pull it off. He's also got a pretty high HP.

ELEMENTAL POWER: 8   **ARMOUR:** Heavy

WARRIOR WISDOM

Phoenician ships were powered by two or even three rows of oars, and protected by marines equipped with spears and swords who would defend the oarsmen and attack the enemy crew.

RARE

ARDO *THE VICIOUS VISIGOTH*

YEAR: 711 AD   **WEAPON:** Long Seax

BIO: Battling invading Umayyad forces in Hispania, Ardo lost his weapon and was forced to smash attackers in the face with his iron helmet. He was relieving himself against a tree when the call of the Wildlands called him in.

SPECIAL MOVE: Ardo's powerful **Team Strike** move deals a huge blow his enemy but also sucks health from his own team. Use wisely.

ELEMENTAL POWER: 2

ARMOUR: Heavy

RARE

LEON *THE BRAWLING GAUL*

YEAR: 52 BC   **WEAPON:** Long Sword

BIO: Quiet but savage, Leon helped defeat the forces of Julius Caesar in the Battle of Gergovia. He was summoned to the Wildlands having just impaled three Roman legionaries on a single spear.

SPECIAL MOVE: **Ice Storm** freezes all his enemies, bringing their health down. He also has the specialist skill Antidote, which means he's more resistant to poison than most warriors. Use Leon in battles against enemies that try to use venomous attacks.

ELEMENTAL POWER: 97

ARMOUR: Medium

SUPER RARE

KASIM
THE OTTOMAN WARRIOR

YEAR: 1453 AD   **WEAPON:** Scimitar

BIO: Bewildered by a lunar eclipse, Kasim got into a fierce tussle with Emperor Constantine himself. Luckily, Kasim was summoned to the Wildlands before landing the final blow.

SPECIAL MOVE: Kasim delivers a deadly **Frozen Crunch**. His elemental rating is high, which will cause any Fire warriors he meets some serious trouble. He's also got the Guard skill, which means he can sometimes escape attacks unscathed.

ELEMENTAL POWER: 56   **ARMOUR:** Medium

SUPER RARE

KWAN *THE HWARANG WARRIOR*

YEAR: 689 AD   **WEAPON:** Geom

BIO: Kwan was once a revered general in 7th century Silla. After receiving an electric shock from a communication kite, he came to his senses in the Wildlands.

SPECIAL MOVE: He helps elemental comrades by providing a **Water Boost**, improving their stats. He's wearing heavy armour – 322 HP as standard – and his Guard skill randomly reduces damage from enemy attacks.

ELEMENTAL POWER: 35   **ARMOUR:** Heavy

JOAN *THE WARRIOR MAID*

YEAR: 1431 AD   **WEAPON:** Epee Batarde

BIO: Captured while attacking Burgundians in the Ardennes, Joan was sentenced to death by burning at the stake. Thankfully, she was summoned to the Wildlands just as the flames began to engulf her.

SPECIAL MOVE: Joan freezes her enemies with the epic **Ice Storm**, and her Soul Spirit skill means her remaining teammates become stronger every time one gets knocked out.

ELEMENTAL POWER: 32

ARMOUR: Medium

MUNGO *THE CELTIC BERSERKER*

YEAR: 218 BC   **WEAPON:** Long Sword

BIO: This crazed Celt was once famed for his frenzied attacks on Roman settlements. Now that he's in the Wildlands, you can harness his power for yourself.

SPECIAL MOVE: His starting HP is an almighty 854, so he'll be able to handle any attack the enemy can throw at him – even the first blow in a fully loaded Puzzle Fight. Then it's time to unleash his **Berserk** move and watch opponents flee in terror.

ELEMENTAL POWER: 91

ARMOUR: Light

KOFI *THE BENIN BODYGUARD*

YEAR: 1468 AD   **WEAPON:** Ada

BIO: Former royal guard Kofi is a loyal but cunning warrior who can crush opponents in just a few moves. Expect no mercy from this fearless fighter – he is at his most dangerous when threatened!

SPECIAL MOVE: Kofi has an unbelievable 1474 HP, and heavy armour – he's practically invincible. Plus, his Antidote skill means poison has less of an effect on him. He's one of the strongest characters to have on your side, and uses **Poison Hive** to take down enemies.

ELEMENTAL POWER: 24

ARMOUR: Heavy

WARRIOR WISDOM

The world's oldest metal suit of armour was found near the ancient Greek city of Mycenae. Made of bronze, around 1400 BC, it's so heavy that its owner probably rode into battle in a chariot.

MANAWA *THE MAORI WARRIOR*

YEAR: 1560 AD   **WEAPON:** Patu

BIO: Performing a haka alongside fellow raiders, Manawa was inches from an enemy warrior's face when he was unceremoniously headbutted. When he came round, he was in the Wildlands.

SPECIAL MOVE: Manawa's **Water Boost** move increases Water damage done by teammates, and he has an incredibly high elemental level, too.

ELEMENTAL POWER: 152

ARMOUR: Light

AGOOLIK *THE INUIT WARRIOR*

YEAR: 1680 AD   **WEAPON:** Stone Axe

BIO: Returning from a hunting trip aboard his trusty dog sled, Agoolik was ambushed by rival tribesmen who left him battered and stranded. He took shelter in an abandoned igloo, but when he emerged at dawn he was lost in the Wildlands.

SPECIAL MOVE: Agoolik's skills need careful planning for best use. His **Phantom Shield** move boosts the armour strength of all team members, and his Retribution skill increases his attack power when he's down to his last 25% of health.

ELEMENTAL POWER: 94   **ARMOUR:** Medium

WALLACE *THE SCOTTISH HIGHLANDER*

YEAR: 1297 AD   **WEAPON:** Claymore

BIO: Charging at retreating English forces with frenzied abandon, Wallace was halfway across Stirling Bridge when it collapsed. He was summoned to the Wildlands just before he drowned.

SPECIAL MOVE: He uses **Bombard** to launch a delayed airstrike, which he can call in at any time, to rain down on whichever enemy is in battle. Perfect for taking out Stealth attackers.

ELEMENTAL POWER: 67   **ARMOUR:** Medium

WARRIOR WISDOM

Inuit hunters, living in the Arctic, super-charged their short driftwood or antler bows by stringing an animal sinew along the back, which increased its strength.

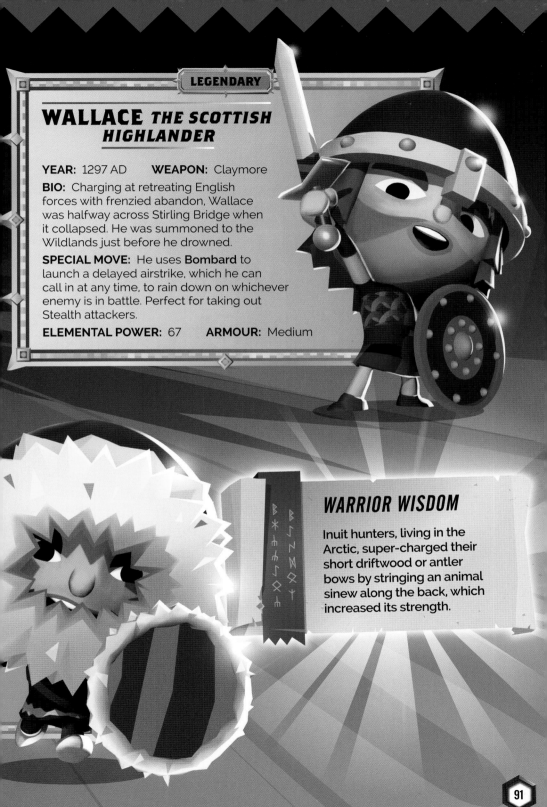

THE CITADEL

THE CITADEL I

You're hot on the trail of the Wildforge now! Shame these three level twenty enemies are standing in your way.

THE CITADEL II

Raze's Phantom Strike will cause your team some serious pain, so equip them with talismans for damage limitation.

THE CITADEL III

A mixed bag of elements awaits you in this battle. Earth, Air and Fire are your foes – pick your warriors accordingly.

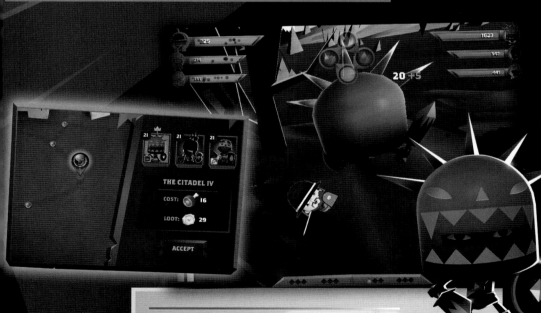

THE CITADEL IV   *PUZZLE FIGHT – Toxic*

Not fair! Gruesome Gobber's Toxic talisman means your warrior will start the battle suffering from poison. Destroy Gobber and save your team from the infection.

THE CITADEL V

Not only are you up against two brutal Fire warriors, but they're also a heavy level twenty-one. Februl's Fire Boost will up the Fire attack of his teammate Flak, too, so don't get caught out.

THE CITADEL VI

Three fearsome foes stand at the very gates of the Citadel. They'll do their best to drain your health and your mana to stop you advancing any further.

THE CITADEL VII   *PUZZLE FIGHT – Meatshield*

While you're bravely chipping away at Dagdoom's incredible 2784 HP, No-Go will be attacking you with Stealth Strike but without tagging into the fight. Use Switch Strike to take him down early.

THE CITADEL VIII

Dark-Dirk will rely on his Regeneration move to push up the health of his Earth warrior comrades, while they batter you with rocks. Use Fire to flush 'em out.

WARRIOR WISDOM

Scythian archers poisoned their arrows with a mixture of snake venom, human blood and dung – the type of stuff the Greeks called toxicon (meaning 'arrow poison') and from which we get the word toxic (poisonous).

THE CITADEL IX

Once again, you'll need to take out No-Go and the sneaky Stealth Strike before you'll have the chance to tussle with the rest of the enemy team.

THE CITADEL X
PUZZLE FIGHT – Mega Armour

Not only are you going to struggle to bash away at Keelok's Mega Armour, but Leech will be restoring his health at the same time. Poison is your best friend here – ideally something that will hurt them both at the same time.

TOP TIP

Some talismans require other talismans as an ingredient. They are consumed in the process, but the new one will be far more powerful.

MATERIALS TO FIND:

 Bronze Ingot

 Silver Ingot

 Gold Ingot

 Almnuts

 Mistwood

BONEBLOOD BRIDGE

BONEBLOOD BRIDGE I

Still got the hunger for battle after the bloody aftermath of the Citadel? Then get stuck into this spooky new realm. Here, two Air warriors and the mysterious Niteskull want to crush you to a pulp.

BONEBLOOD BRIDGE II

These three tough guys are all level twenty-three. Can your warriors match up? If you've trained up all your current fighters as far as possible, try the Temple to call down a Legendary fighter.

BONEBLOOD BRIDGE III — *PUZZLE FIGHT – Fully Loaded*

Grumble starts the fight with full mana, and his Apocalypto special move is devastating. But, if you can survive his initial move, he'll fall easily enough.

BONEBLOOD BRIDGE IV

These three members of the Skull Army would like nothing more than to stop you in your tracks. Sneek's Claw Crush move is brutal against Air warriors, so keep them on the bench.

BONEBLOOD BRIDGE V

The last battle of this short realm sees you taking on two Earth and one Fire warrior, but they're a hard-hitting level twenty-four. If you're falling short, try going back and redoing some earlier fights to earn XP and level up your own fighters.

BONEBLOOD BRIDGE VI   *PUZZLE FIGHT – Elemental Teams*

The other side of the bridge's gate holds a trio of Water enemies to test your mettle. Equip your most powerful Air warrior with a damage talisman, and you'll see them off.

BONEBLOOD BRIDGE VII

It's another jump in enemy strength, up to level twenty-five. Driz's Ice Storm will do damage to your whole team, so bring in a warrior that can regenerate the team's health.

BONEBLOOD BRIDGE VIII

Depending on your level of experience, you should have enough meat to see you through these last few battles. If not, spend some stones to recharge, or wait it out.

WARRIOR WISDOM

In 261 BC, in one of the bloodiest battles ever, more than 250,000 people died when Ashoka, emperor of India's Mauryan Empire, defeated the state of Kalinga using chariots, elephants, infantry and archers.

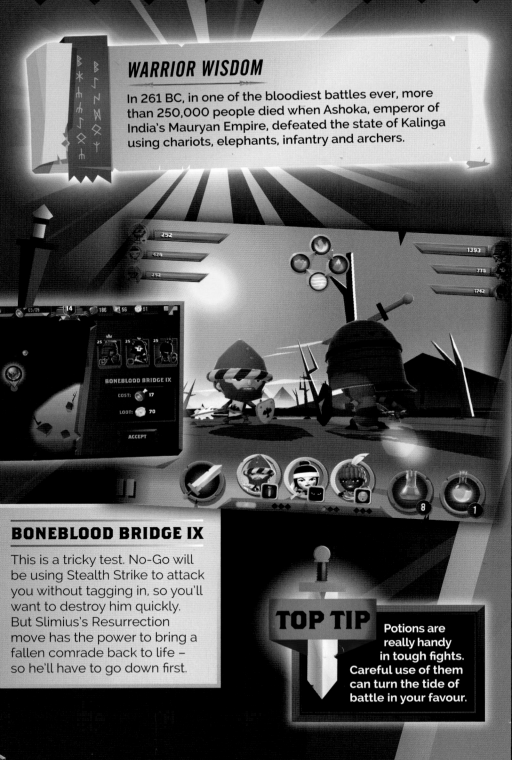

BONEBLOOD BRIDGE IX

This is a tricky test. No-Go will be using Stealth Strike to attack you without tagging in, so you'll want to destroy him quickly. But Slimius's Resurrection move has the power to bring a fallen comrade back to life – so he'll have to go down first.

TOP TIP

Potions are really handy in tough fights. Careful use of them can turn the tide of battle in your favour.

BOSS FIGHT

BONEBLOOD BRIDGE X

Lagoonus is the Skull Boss to beat here. He's holding an Elemental Shield, which means you'll need your heaviest hitters to take him down. Good thing, too, as he's got a whopping 2523 HP.

BONEBLOOD BRIDGE X

COST: 20

LOOT: 75

ACCEPT

MATERIALS TO FIND:

 Bronze Ingot
 Silver Ingot
 Gold Ingot
 Mistwood
 Toadthrone

MICKLEMUCK MARSHES

MICKLEMUCK MARSHES I

There are only two enemies in your first battle here. Good thing, too – this Fire and Air combo is a tricky one.

MICKLEMUCK MARSHES II

Your next step, as you pick your way through the Bog of Bones, is to destroy these Skull Army fighters. Shokka's Thunder Strike will be catastrophic to Air warriors.

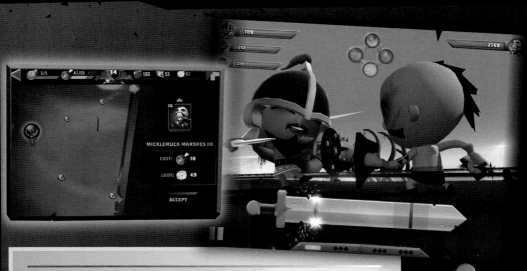

MICKLEMUCK MARSHES III *PUZZLE FIGHT – Bomb*

You should have the hang of these by now. Bring in your most powerful fighters and destroy Dungo before he has the chance to charge up his mana and unleash his unstoppable special attack.

MICKLEMUCK MARSHES IV

Krukk loves nothing more than using Switch Strike to pick away at your warriors until they drop dead. Use his own move against him!

MICKLEMUCK MARSHES V

Not only are there three enemies to vanquish here, but they're also a higher level – twenty-seven. You'll want to do something about SirPent as early as possible to avoid poisoning.

MICKLEMUCK MARSHES VI *PUZZLE FIGHT – Toxic*

Speaking of poison, in this fight your players will slowly succumb to a venom attack for as long as Gobber is alive. In battle, hit the blue potion bottle for a mana refill, and take him down with special moves.

MICKLEMUCK MARSHES VII

The good news is that the lead enemy in this battle won't give an elemental boost to his teammates. The bad news is all three of them are a fearsome level twenty-eight.

MICKLEMUCK MARSHES VIII

In the dark and spooky marshes, dark and spooky moves are used – like Resurrection and Drain. Beware!

MICKLEMUCK MARSHES IX

Try equipping your warriors with different talismans – new combinations can sometimes be more powerful.

WARRIOR WISDOM

Ravens appeared on Viking flags and boats because it was believed that birds that looked for dead animals resembled the spirits who carried dead warriors to heaven.

BOSS FIGHT

MICKLEMUCK MARSHES X

Keelok is wearing a Mega Armour talisman, which means you'll need to use elemental power to take him down. The bad guys are all Air, so call on as many powerful Earth warriors as you can.

PUZZLE FIGHT –
Elemental Teams

MATERIALS TO FIND:

 Bronze Ingot

 Silver Ingot

 Gold Ingot

 Toadthrone

 Skull Rune

BLACK GAUNTLET

BLACK GAUNTLET I

Don't say you weren't warned about the sandy wasteland that lies ahead. Or the three level twenty-nine foes waiting to send you back where you came from . . .

BLACK GAUNTLET II

Not one but two versions of Niteskull are here to crack your head open – one Fire and one Water. They'll both try to drain your mana.

BLACK GAUNTLET III *PUZZLE FIGHT – Bomb*

Uh-oh, the maniac Dungo is back for more! If he racks up enough mana, he'll blow up your entire team. Use powerful Earth warriors to make sure he doesn't get that far.

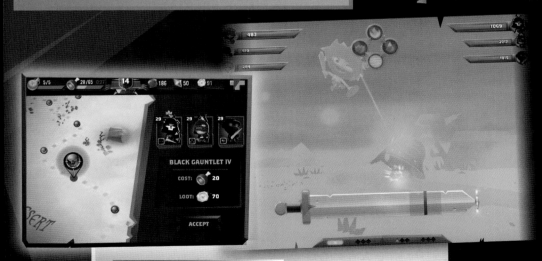

BLACK GAUNTLET IV

No-Go will be flitting in and out to attack you while his cronies fill up his health monitor. The way to win? Use attacks that hurt the whole team at once.

BLACK GAUNTLET V

Don't be fooled into thinking that this pair will be easier than a trio – they're both level thirty, and Slimius has the power to bring his pals back from the dead.

BLACK GAUNTLET VI *PUZZLE FIGHT – Fully Loaded*

Try and withstand Grumble's ferocious Apocalypto move. If you can survive the initial wave, he's yours for the taking.

WEAK

BLACK GAUNTLET VII

Mudd's Boulder Bash special move will crush your entire team, so try and knock him down early to save your warriors' health.

BLACK GAUNTLET VIII

Just two enemies to face here: a pair of level thirty-one thugs. Take in Earth and Air warriors of your own for maximum elemental efficiency.

BLACK GAUNTLET IX

Once again, you're up against a deadly duo: MadKat and Leech. The former will battle to wipe away your health, and the latter will keep his teammates' health high.

WARRIOR WISDOM

For centuries, merchants crossing the sands of the Sahara were attacked by Tuareg desert warriors, who tied a stone to their right arm to build up their strength for sword-fighting.

BOSS FIGHT

BLACK GAUNTLET X

Look out! It's a new and dangerous enemy. Say hello to Skull Boss RedBlade, whose talisman allows him to regenerate health while he's not in the ring. He's a Fire warrior, so use Water to extinguish his flames.

MATERIALS TO FIND:

 Bronze Ingot   Silver Ingot   Gold Ingot   Toadthrone   Skull Rune

AIR WARRIORS

Air warriors have the power to send their enemies into a spin and keep themselves out of harm's way when a quick escape is needed. Their elemental force is strongest against Water warriors, who just can't handle the tornado.

COMMON

SAKUMA *THE LONE SAMURAI*

YEAR: 1397 AD   **WEAPON:** Katana

BIO: Before his destiny led him to the Wildlands, Sakuma was banished from his clan for breaking the Samurai code, disobeying orders and slicing off his master's head.

SPECIAL MOVE: Phantom Strike inflicts high physical damage to all enemies. Sakuma is the best bet in battles where elemental damage isn't so important and his brute force can do all the talking.

ELEMENTAL POWER: 7   **ARMOUR:** Heavy

WARRIOR WISDOM

A samurai's face-mask was often lacquered red and its features were shaped into the angry stare of a demon, complete with horsehair moustache – to make the warrior look as scary as possible.

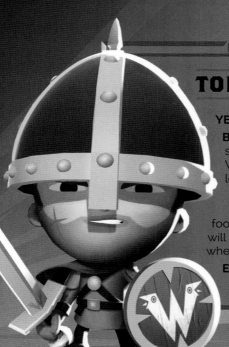

TOKI *THE VIKING WARRIOR*

YEAR: 787 AD   **WEAPON:** Long Sword

BIO: Famed for his heroism and swordsmanship, Toki was called to the Wildlands as he leapt from his blazing longship during a calamitous dawn raid.

SPECIAL MOVE: Tornado Strike is a whirling banshee of pain for any enemy foolish enough to be caught in it – and it will damage the whole opposition team when used.

ELEMENTAL POWER: 18

ARMOUR: Light

CRIXUS *THE ROMAN GLADIATOR*

YEAR: 112 AD   **WEAPON:** Trident

BIO: Having escaped from the Colosseum by hiding in a cart full of mangled corpses, this gladiator thought his fighting days were finally over before he was summoned to the Wildlands.

SPECIAL MOVE: Air Boost helps to improve the elemental damage inflicted by all Air team members, so it's a handy ally in a battle against Water warriors. Crixus can also reduce Earth damage by 15% when he's in the Leader position. He's a real elemental powerhouse!

ELEMENTAL POWER: 23   **ARMOUR:** Heavy

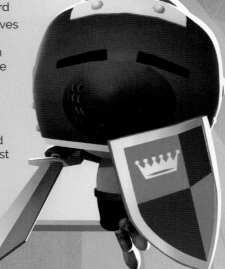

HANNIBAL
THE CARTHAGINIAN GENERAL

YEAR: 218 BC   **WEAPON:** Falcata

BIO: Hannibal was crossing the Alps during the second Punic War when boulders blocked his path. He tried to fracture the rock using vinegar and fire, but instead he vanished to the Wildlands in a flash of blue light!

SPECIAL MOVE: Hannibal is master of the **Bombard** move, which calls in a heavy yet delayed air strike on whichever opponent is on screen. It's worth the wait, as it'll cause some heavy-duty physical damage.

ELEMENTAL POWER: 9   **ARMOUR:** Heavy

SUPER RARE

FURIO *THE FLORENTINE KNIGHT*

YEAR: 1399 AD   **WEAPON:** Italian Sword

BIO: Furio is a ferocious warrior who also loves wine, women and song. He was sentenced to death for accidentally disembowelling an enraged husband but was summoned to the Wildlands just before the axe fell.

SPECIAL MOVE: Furio's fearsome **Team Strike** move does massive damage to the enemy, but draws health from his entire team to charge its power. Never to be used when warriors are feeling weak, Furio is best for starting fights, not ending them.

ELEMENTAL POWER: 18

ARMOUR: Heavy

ERIKA *THE VIKING SHIELD MAIDEN*

YEAR: 621 AD   **WEAPON:** Long Sword

BIO: Fiery-tempered Erika was summoned to the Wildlands in the middle of wreaking blood-spattered mayhem against her Viking shipmates, who mocked her for showing mercy to a kidnapped priest.

SPECIAL MOVE: Tempest is one of the most powerful Air moves to be found, and it damages the entire opposition team with a massive elemental blast. Erika can also inflict random extra damage with her Critical Hit skill. This Viking Shield Maiden is a real wildcard!

ELEMENTAL POWER: 63   **ARMOUR:** Medium

WU *THE SHAOLIN MONK*

YEAR: 1379 AD   **WEAPON:** Jian

BIO: Before being transported to the Wildlands, Wu commanded a ruthless mercenary strike force from a mountaintop monastery in central China. He is renowned for his stealth and mystical healing powers.

SPECIAL MOVE: Wu can use **Regeneration** to gradually refuel the health of all his team members, so keep him alive as long as possible. The team also receives 30% less Air damage when he's in charge.

ELEMENTAL POWER: 54   **ARMOUR:** Light

LEGENDARY

KURO *THE MIDNIGHT NINJA*

YEAR: 1579 AD   **WEAPON:** Chokutō

BIO: Master of stealth, Kuro has refused to remove his black garb ever since he arrived in the Wildlands. Rumours abound that he is the mysterious Ninja warrior who was last spotted scaling Azuchi Castle to assassinate a notorious Japanese warlord.

SPECIAL MOVE: Kuro can cause damage without tagging into the fight by using **Stealth Strike**, which suits his sneaky personality perfectly. He also has the Retribution skill, which increases his attack power when reduced to his final 25% of health.

ELEMENTAL POWER: 20   **ARMOUR:** Light

LEGENDARY

HELIOS *THE MACEDONIAN WARRIOR*

YEAR: 330 BC   **WEAPON:** Kopis Sword

BIO: Helios never did find out who won the Battle of the Persian Gate. Trapped on a narrow mountain pass, as Persian forces rained down boulders, he slipped into an icy ravine and found himself in the Wildlands.

SPECIAL MOVE: **Team Strike** allows Helios to use his own team's health to inflict a heavy blow on the opposition. His rare Guard and Soul Spirit skills reduce damage from enemy attacks and strengthen his teammates after he's been knocked out.

ELEMENTAL POWER: 18

ARMOUR: Heavy

UTU *THE SUMERIAN WARRIOR*

YEAR: 2495 BC   **WEAPON:** Short Sword

BIO: Patrolling the walled city of Uruk after dark, Utu was set upon by thugs who tried to steal his ceremonial dagger. Utu would have torn them limb from limb had he not been summoned to the Wildlands at that moment.

SPECIAL MOVE: Utu's **Air Boost** helps his team by increasing the Air damage inflicted by all team members – so when it's time to take down Water warriors, you should pick him first.

ELEMENTAL POWER: 117

ARMOUR: Medium

PING *THE TANG DYNASTY PRINCESS*

YEAR: 623 AD   **WEAPON:** Jian

BIO: Ping was attacked at an Imperial banquet in Chang'an by an infatuated servant with a sharpened chopstick. The princess deflected the blow and tumbled beneath the table, only to find herself in the Wildlands.

SPECIAL MOVE: An elemental master, Ping uses **Tempest** to blast all enemies with a hefty dose of Air. Plus, she has the Mana Spring skill, which occasionally spawns extra mana when hit – thus creating more chances to use Tempest.

ELEMENTAL POWER: 120

ARMOUR: Medium

RITHALIM'S BASTION

RITHALIM'S BASTION I

This is a massive step up in difficulty – straight in against three enemies who are all level thirty-two with a mixture of elements. Sneek's Claw Crush is the most dangerous move you'll face here.

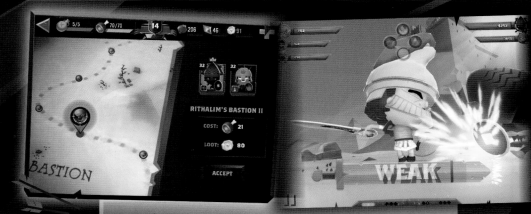

RITHALIM'S BASTION II

Now this is more like it! There are just two foes here. A combination of Air and Fire enemies means you should send in Earth and Water warriors to tackle them. Just make sure you don't get them mixed up.

RITHALIM'S BASTION III

Time to get down and dirty against two Earth warriors that are all about regaining health. Burn 'em up with a powerful Fire warrior, then pick off SirPent at your leisure.

RITHALIM'S BASTION IV

PUZZLE FIGHT – Elemental Immunity

Watch out! Frakus has a powerful talisman in his Elemental Shield. Added to that, his buddy Leech will keep topping up his health with Healing power. Use big hitters to take Leech out, then plug away at Frakus.

RITHALIM'S BASTION V

Conjunctus will use Mimic to perform a special move belonging to a random member of your side. So don't load up with the same element, as it might end up causing you catastrophic team damage.

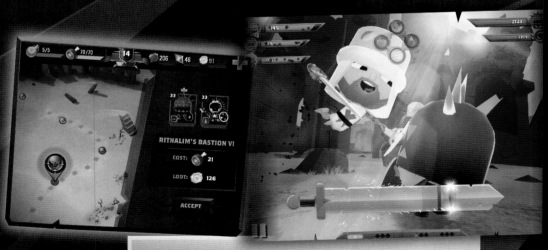

RITHALIM'S BASTION VI

Frakus is back with his Elemental Shield, and he's even deadlier now he's got Gobber to back him up. Remember, it's no use trying to use the elements to hurt Frakus, so send in your most powerful warriors.

RITHALIM'S BASTION VII *PUZZLE FIGHT – Meatshield*

This is a really tricky one! Dagdoom's incredible HP means he'll take some wearing down, and No-Go will be damaging you with Stealth Strike without tagging in. Plus, Gobber's toxicity will poison your team. Use Switch Strike to target No-Go first.

RITHALIM'S BASTION VIII

As you're up against level thirty-four enemies now, it may be time to retire to the Home Camp and train up any warriors you have that can be improved. The more trained up they are, the harder they'll be to take down.

RITHALIM'S BASTION IX

Ded-Fang and Ooze are both powerful Water warriors. Ooze will use Water Boost to bump up their elemental damage. So try and take him down before he amasses enough mana to unleash it.

WARRIOR WISDOM

Roman slaves dressed as the god Mercury tested fallen gladiators by poking them with a red-hot iron rod to see if they were actually dead or just pretending.

BOSS FIGHT

RITHALIM'S BASTION X

Three slimy Earth warriors guard your passage to the next section. Knock Rok out early so he can't use Earth Boost, then start using as many Fire attacks as possible to combat their element.

MATERIALS TO FIND:

 Bronze Ingot   Silver Ingot   Gold Ingot   Toadthrone   Skull Rune

RED RIVER RIFT

WEAK

RED RIVER RIFT I

Even if you take down Fester quickly, his sinister partner Slimius can use Resurrection to bring him back to life. Make sure Slimius falls first.

RED RIVER RIFT II

Can you handle three enemies, each at level thirty-five? If not, visit the Temple to try and call down some more Legendary warriors. You'll need them to resist Wurmslime's Soul Steal move.

WEAK

RED RIVER RIFT III *PUZZLE FIGHT – Mega Armour*

Keelok is sporting Mega Armour, which means you'll need serious elemental power to take him down. Be wary though: Slimius might just resurrect him as soon as you do. Once again, the key to winning is to destroy him first.

WARRIOR WISDOM

Cataphracts, the core of the Armenian cavalry, were heavily-armoured mounted warriors, who wore chainmail and were armed with a lance – which they gripped with both hands when galloping at an enemy army.

RED RIVER RIFT IV

With Dark-Dirk in the Leader position, this band of three Skull Warriors won't go down without a fight. Yet again, Slimius will be a thorn in your side so you should target him first.

RED RIVER RIFT V

Don't put any Earth warriors in your roster for this fight – Flak's Fire Storm move, coupled with his 150 elemental power, will see them reduced to cinders.

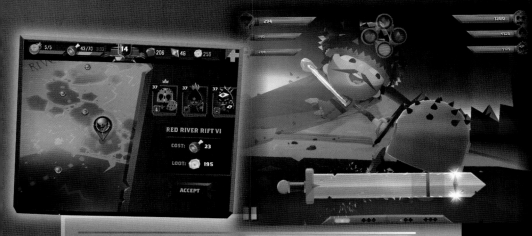

RED RIVER RIFT VI *PUZZLE FIGHT – Elemental Teams*

Three level thirty-seven Fire fighters to face down. But as long as you've got plenty of healing talismans equipped and high-powered Water warriors on your side, you'll be fine.

WARRIOR WISDOM

When Persian ships attacked Greece in 480 BC, Hydna – a Greek female diver – and her father swam out through stormy waters and cut the vessels' anchor ropes, leaving them to collide and sink.

RED RIVER RIFT VII

It's not a surprise that Fire warriors seem to hang out in this volcanic wasteland. Luckily, the only one in this fight would rather heal his teammates than destroy yours.

WARRIOR WISDOM

The Huns got a head-start in warfare by tightly wrapping layers of wood and cloth around children's heads until their skulls became longer, flatter and scarier by the time they grew up.

BOSS
FIGHT

RED RIVER RIFT VIII

Nobody said saving the Wildlands was easy. Prepare to take on three Skull Army bosses. BoarHammer, RamRaider and Obsidiux haven't gotten any easier since you last faced them. You'll have to play around with tactics and line-ups before you will prevail here.

MATERIALS TO FIND:

 Bronze Ingot   Silver Ingot   Gold Ingot   Toadthrone   Skull Rune

FEVERED FALLS

FEVERED FALLS I

You've come a long way and now command an epic army of warriors, which is good as you are going to need them for what lies ahead of you in Fevered Falls! Your first match sees a mix of elements, so choose your fighters carefully.

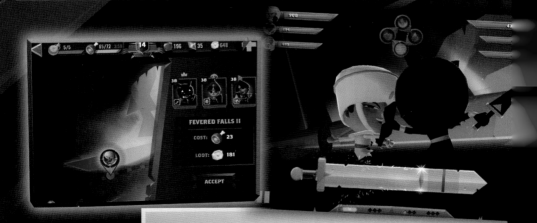

FEVERED FALLS II

MadKat leads these Skull Army warriors, and his Berserker move will do you some serious damage. Equip your warriors with high HP to absorb the attack.

FEVERED FALLS III

Two Earth enemies sandwich a Fire warrior here – so you'll want to mix and match. Two Fire and one Water should see you right. Switch them in and out to match the enemy.

FEVERED FALLS IV   *PUZZLE FIGHT – Meatshield*

Can you outsmart the enemy's tactics? You'll notice that No-Go isn't tagging into the battle, so you'll have to bring the fight to him using Switch Strike.

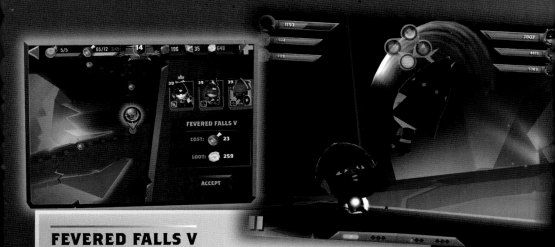

FEVERED FALLS V

The enemies are at level thirty-nine now, the fiercest you will have faced so far. Shokka, in the Leader position, has a colossal 3978 HP. She has no talismans to help her, though.

FEVERED FALLS VI   *PUZZLE FIGHT – Elemental Teams*

You're up against two Air enemies here, strong ones too. Raze has a massive 6780 HP, so you'll want to use a warrior with a high elemental power in the Earth category.

FEVERED FALLS VII — *PUZZLE FIGHT – Fully Loaded*

Another Puzzle Fight straight after the last one! Fevered Falls is a seriously harsh environment. Make sure you withstand Grumble's powerful Apocalypto move and he'll fall soon after.

FEVERED FALLS VIII

You face a mix of opponents here. Be smart with how you set your team up, because there are no easy elemental winnings to be found in this place.

FEVERED FALLS IX

Brrr! Feel that chill? It's Driz's Ice Storm move and it has the power to freeze your whole team solid. Also watch out for Gruft as he'll try to hurt your whole army when he uses his special mana move.

WARRIOR WISDOM

In 2012, sixteen severed hands were discovered in an ancient Egyptian palace. Egyptian soldiers had to provide evidence of the number of enemies they had killed or captured in order to be paid.

FEVERED FALLS X *PUZZLE FIGHT – Elemental Teams*

This won't be easy. Level forty-one enemies, all Water warriors, headed up by Frakus who is also holding an Elemental Shield. Some huge hitters are required to survive here. Spend some Wildstones on super powered warriors before entering the battlefield.

FEVERED FALLS X

COST: 23

LOOT: 389

ACCEPT

MATERIALS TO FIND:

 Bronze Ingot   Silver Ingot   Gold Ingot   Skull Rune   Ether Wine

EARTH WARRIORS

Behold the mighty Earth warriors! They use their awesome elemental power to bludgeon, bash and crush their foes into the dirt. However they are weakest against Fire fighters so use them wisely.

COMMON

GUNNAR
THE VIKING RAIDER

YEAR: 798 AD   **WEAPON:** Long Sword

BIO: Summoned to the Wildlands shortly after looting three monasteries in two days, Gunnar is convinced he is now living in Valhalla.

SPECIAL MOVE: Vikings were renowned for their fierceness, and Gunnar's out-of-control **Berserk** move might be why. It costs him health, but not as much as his foe.

ELEMENTAL POWER: 4   **ARMOUR:** Heavy

COMMON

OSGOOD THE SAXON DESTROYER

YEAR: 535 AD   **WEAPON:** Long Sword

BIO: Thanks to his exploits battling the forces of King Arthur, Osgood was already a living legend when he eviscerated a dozen traitors in Britannia. He was summoned to the Wildlands while sleeping off a hornful of potent mead.

SPECIAL MOVE: **Boulder Bash** is a terrific move for dealing death to multiple foes. Most effectively used early and often, this Saxon Destroyer loves using it against a full team of three enemies.

ELEMENTAL POWER: 13   **ARMOUR:** Medium

BLAINE *THE GAELIC KERN*

YEAR: 1388 AD   **WEAPON:** Sparth Axe

BIO: Swift and ferocious, Blaine misses the days before the Wildlands when he would gallop away from cattle raids with a few severed heads dangling from his horse's saddle.

SPECIAL MOVE: Every team needs a Blaine – someone who can use **Regeneration** to gradually restore health to all team members. He's not the flashiest of fighters but he won't let you down.

ELEMENTAL POWER: 10

ARMOUR: Heavy

RARE

JIN *THE MING WARRIOR*

YEAR: 1472 AD   **WEAPON:** Jian

BIO: Jin spent many years battling barbarians during the peak of the Ming Dynasty, and was whisked away to the Wildlands just before a royal audience in the Forbidden City.

SPECIAL MOVE: **Phantom Strike** allows Jin to pick and choose which enemy he attacks. It's perfect for taking down opponents who are trying to hang back. There's no hiding from Jin's retribution!

ELEMENTAL POWER: 11

ARMOUR: Medium

AKA *THE ZANDE WARRIOR*

YEAR: 1474 AD **WEAPON:** Makraka Sword

BIO: Aka became convinced he was destined for greatness following a vision in which he saw himself battling gleaming monsters with metal skin. Since his call to the Wildlands, his dreams are coming true.

SPECIAL MOVE: **Claw Crush** is one of the game's most powerful moves. Aka uses it to pick his hapless opponents up in a rocky grip, and then crush them to the floor, shattering their bones.

ELEMENTAL POWER: 26 **ARMOUR:** Light

RARE

LANCE *THE KNIGHT TEMPLAR*

YEAR: 1177 AD **WEAPON:** Arming Sword

BIO: Laying waste to Saladin's dwindling troops during the epic battle of Montgisard, Lance was momentarily distracted by the Sultan fleeing on a racing camel. Before he could pursue him, Lance was summoned to the Wildlands.

SPECIAL MOVE: Lance's **Thunder Strike** electrocutes enemies with the power of lightning. It requires fast fingers to get the all-important perfect blow, but when he manages it, just watch those enemies fry.

ELEMENTAL POWER: 5 **ARMOUR:** Heavy

WARRIOR WISDOM

At the Battle of Montgisard (1177), just eighty Knights Templar, heavily-armed shock troops of the Crusaders, smashed into the enemy frontline like medieval tanks, breaking up an Arab army of 26,000 men.

SHAKA
THE ZULU WARRIOR

YEAR: 1820 AD   **WEAPON:** Iklwa

BIO: A formidable warrior, Shaka was returning home from an initiation ceremony when he thought he saw a female hand beckoning him through a waterfall. Baffled but curious, he plunged through, only to find himself trapped in the Wildlands.

SPECIAL MOVE: With Shaka, the element of surprise is everything. His special move is one that is randomly selected every time. He's another wildcard, but might not always pull out the best move for the occasion.

ELEMENTAL POWER: 16   **ARMOUR:** Light

SUPER RARE

RAVI *THE MAURYAN WARRIOR*

YEAR: 263 AD

WEAPON: Khanda Sword

BIO: Renowned for his ability to fell three men with a single blow, this marauding Mauryan was summoned to the Wildlands as he trampled enemy archers astride his trusty war elephant during the Kalinga War.

SPECIAL MOVE: Ravi can use the sneaky **Switch Strike** to target specific members of the opposing team. This will come in very handy when picking off a hiding warrior with just a few HP left.

ELEMENTAL POWER: 15   **ARMOUR:** Light

KUKAN *THE MAYAN WARRIOR*

YEAR: 1531 AD   **WEAPON:** Club

BIO: Clambering down a jungle vine into a yawning limestone sinkhole, Kukan was certain he'd escaped the traitors planning to sell him to Conquistadors. Unfortunately the vine was cut and Kukan fell into darkness, landing in the Wildlands.

SPECIAL MOVE: Poison Dart is deadly, accurate and toxic to any member of the opposing team. The venom works over more than one turn, so if enemies reckon they're safe when Kukan's move is over, they should think again.

ELEMENTAL POWER: 31

ARMOUR: Light

SPURIUS
THE ETRUSCAN WARRIOR

YEAR: 351 BC   **WEAPON:** Xiphos

BIO: Visiting the Bay of Naples for peace talks, Spurius was planning to slay as many Roman negotiators as possible the second things turned sour. But he was spirited away to the Wildlands while chopping only his eighth envoy to bits.

SPECIAL MOVE: Spurius is one of the most powerful Earth warriors, and **Earth Boost** gives all his teammates an elemental leg-up. Great for Elemental Team Puzzle Fights, or just slapping down pesky Air fighters.

ELEMENTAL POWER: 114

ARMOUR: Medium

DOONGARA *THE AUSTRALIAN ABORIGINE*

YEAR: 1400 AD   **WEAPON:** Mulga Wood Club

BIO: Returning home from a coming-of-age ceremony beneath Uluru, Doongara was stung by a scorpion lurking in his didgeridoo. Delirious, he staggered into the Outback and picked up an amulet, which whisked him away to the Wildlands.

SPECIAL MOVE: **Claw Crush** is a guaranteed way to reduce an enemy's HP to zero. Plus. Doongara has the Auto Potion skill, which is like carrying extra HP into battle for himself and means he can self-medicate as he fights!

ELEMENTAL POWER: 174   **ARMOUR:** Light

RODRIGO
THE CASTILIAN WARRIOR

YEAR: 1099 AD   **WEAPON:** Tizona

BIO: A revered nobleman, Rodrigo was defending Valencia from marauding Berbers when his horse began to act strangely. Noticing a golden talisman glistening in the beast's fresh manure, he picked it up and was summoned to the Wildlands.

SPECIAL MOVE: **Bombard** calls a delayed airstrike on whichever opponent is on screen, and the Soul Spirit skill means Rodrigo's teammates get stronger after he's knocked out. So sometimes losing him can be a good thing!

ELEMENTAL POWER: 70   **ARMOUR:** Heavy

WARRIOR WISDOM

After ten years of war, Spanish soldiers from the Kingdom of Castile finally captured the fortress-city of Granada in 1492, using cannons and early types of guns called arquebuses.

THE SKULL ARMY

The Wildlands are awash with bandits, bullies and thugs, all in the pay of King Boneshaker. Together they form the Skull Army, a bloodthirsty band of fighters that want to destroy everyone in their path, so it's important that you get to know your enemy. Some will try to leech the life out of you with deadly poison, while others will try to hack you to pieces with axes and swords, or tear you limb from limb with their bare hands. While every battle will be different, the Skull Army have one thing in common — a lust for warrior blood!

SKULL ARMY MINIONS

BLUDBEARD
THE BLAZING BATTLER

Originally from Volcano Canyon, BludBeard fell under King Boneshaker's influence and defected to the Skull Army after swallowing a Fire Charm during the notorious Battle of Sulpurnius.

WEAPON: Scorch Shield

ELEMENT: Fire

SPECIAL MOVE: BludBeard's **Inferno** move will send Earth warriors running for cover.

DED-FANG
OF THE WOLFGUARD

Rumoured to have slain the giant wolf whose pelt he wears with his bare hands, Ded-Fang is exceptionally ferocious, with a bark that is just as bad as his bite!

WEAPON: Fang Club

ELEMENT: Varies

SPECIAL MOVE: **Team Strike** will cause a devastating blow to the opposition team, but at the cost of some of his own team's health.

SLYDOR
THE TIDE RAIDER

Once a respected commander in the formidable Ice Legion, Slydor could not resist enlisting in the Skull Army after witnessing its awesome power during the Sea Forge Siege. Now a fully paid-up servant of evil, this sneaky defector is a savage opponent on land or sea.

WEAPON: Ice Javelin

ELEMENT: Water

SPECIAL MOVE: Frozen Crunch encases Slydor's adversary in ice, before he smashes them back out with a mighty blow.

DRIZ
THE MASTER OF GLUGORUS

Able to wreak havoc via the power of Water, Driz swore allegiance to the Skull Army in exchange for huge swathes of the Endless Oceans.

WEAPON: Riptide Axe

ELEMENT: Water

SPECIAL MOVE: Ice Storm freezes Driz's enemies, leaving him to smash into them at his own pace. Avoid at all costs.

FESTER
THE TOXIC TROOPER

Emerging from the noxious Swamps of Ick, following a humiliating dunking at the hands of spiteful locals, Fester decided to use his newfound toxicity to assist the Skull Army.

WEAPON: Lop Sickle

ELEMENT: Earth

SPECIAL MOVE: Fester inflicts damage to all the opposition by using **Poison Hive**, which sends toxic bees out to sting his enemies.

LEECH
THE NOXIOUS LURKER

Leech's identity remains a complete mystery as he refuses to remove his menacing metal gas mask, which is just as well because his face is said to resemble a melted gargoyle.

WEAPON: Lurgy Longsword

ELEMENT: Varies

SPECIAL MOVE: For once, this enemy's special move won't cause you damage, but Leech's **Healing** power will help his own side.

KRUKK
THE BLADE RAIDER

Krukk's fearsome reputation is a direct result of the Battle of Bonehenge. He ordered his troops to surrender, then annihilated the enemy in a sneak attack while the peace treaty was still drying.

WEAPON: Ribcage Rapier

ELEMENT: Varies

SPECIAL MOVE: Crafty Krukk uses **Switch Strike** to target weak opposition, even if they're not tagged into battle.

NITESKULL
THE OBSIDIAN OVERLORD

Originally an assassin-for-hire, Niteskull is now a fearsome Skull Army commander. He is notorious for his spine-chilling cackle and complete lack of compassion.

WEAPON: Midnight Machete

ELEMENT: Varies

SPECIAL MOVE: Just when his foes think they've stored up enough mana for a special, Niteskull uses **Drain** to suck it away and fill his own metre.

151

NO-GO
THE STEALTH MASTER

Many believe No-Go hails from another realm. This may or may not be true but one thing is for sure, he is a brutally efficient fighter whose ability to appear from nowhere is truly terrifying!

WEAPON: Wazikashi

ELEMENT: Varies

SPECIAL MOVE: **Stealth Strike** is just one of the ways that No-Go is a sneaky foe. He can strike out without even tagging into the fight.

SHOKKA
THE STORM ENFORCER

Electrifying in battle, Shokka strikes fear into enemies thanks to her ability to harness the power of lightning, a sinister talent she is thought to have stolen from a warlock she seduced.

WEAPON: Thunder Blade

ELEMENT: Varies

SPECIAL MOVE: Using her huge Thunder Blade, Shokka unleashes a furious **Thunder Strike** on her aggressor, electrocuting them mercilessly.

RAZE
THE FIRESQUAD PHANTOM

A royal bodyguard with a bloodcurdling reputation, Raze is a founding member of the fearsome Firesquad, a shadowy force of callous ex-criminals famed for their blind loyalty to King Boneshaker.

WEAPON: Fire Blade

ELEMENT: Varies

SPECIAL MOVE: Raze is a ferocious foe who can hurt the entire opposition force by using **Phantom Strike**. He must be stopped.

SIRPENT
THE VENOMOUS VANQUISHER

Once a warlock specializing in deadly potions, SirPent is said to have enlisted in the Skull Army when Boneshaker's henchman Lagoonus poisoned his mind with promises of riches.

WEAPON: Forked Flail

ELEMENT: Varies

SPECIAL MOVE: Calling on an army of archers, SirPent bombards his prey with a flurry of **poisoned arrows**, slowly sapping their health.

SKULL ARMY BOSSES

SLICE AND DICE

Don't be fooled by their beguiling looks and flirtatious taunts. Slice and Dice are King Boneshaker's chief assassins. These deadly twins earned their nicknames because of the brutal way in which they dispatch victims.

WEAPONS: Matching Katanas

ELEMENTS: Water and Earth

SPECIAL MOVES: Slice can use **Mimic** to copy another warrior's special move at random. It's devastating if paired up with an elemental move. Dice doesn't like to see her sister in trouble, so uses **Healing** to restore her health in tag-team matches.

LAGOONUS

An early convert to Boneshaker's twisted philosophies, this treacherous warlord is desperate to please his master, no matter what the human cost.

WEAPON: Steel Teeth

ELEMENT: Water

SPECIAL MOVE: Drain sucks away any fighter foolish enough to face Lagoonus's mana. His Elemental Shield talisman means he's protected against elemental damage.

TOP TIP

Before battles, check the enemy's statistics by tapping on them to check which of your warriors is right for the fight ahead.

WARRIOR WISDOM

Aboriginal warriors sometimes used magic spells such as attacking the image of an enemy drawn on the ground. Victims of the legendary 'bone-pointing' curse are known to have died of fear.

DREAM TEAMS

As you travel on your epic journey through the Wildlands, the challenges you face will get increasingly difficult and your enemies will become tougher and tougher to beat. Building a mighty army is absolutely essential to your success and survival.

The following three Dream Teams are the most powerful combinations of warriors to be found in the Wildlands. If you can put these super squads together, you'll be ready for anything and anyone. You'll be unstoppable!

TEAM ONE: SUPER STRIKE

ZUMA (Fire) **ZAHRA** (Air) **DOONGARA** (Earth)

BEST FOR: Taking down opponents with super strong HP, or Mega Armour.

Sometimes elemental power isn't enough – you need clever tactics as well. Zuma's poison arrows will leave a lasting impression on the enemy, while Zahra can use Switch Strike to pick off weaker enemies that may use Revive. Doongara's Claw Crush is a guaranteed hit when it comes to knocking down enemy health levels.

TEAM TWO: ENDURANCE ELITE

KOFI (Water)   **BIBI** (Air)   **RODRIGO** (Earth)

BEST FOR: Long-haul battles.

When you come up against enemies that seem to last forever, you have to match them. Bibi can use Healing to help ailing team mates, Rodrigo's Soul Spirit move strengthens his allies after he's knocked out, and Kofi's high HP makes him really difficult for opponents to finish off.

TEAM THREE: WILD CARDS

PING (Air)   **SPURIUS** (Earth)   **HECTOR** (Fire)

BEST FOR: Elemental Mixtures.

The one thing these three Legendary warriors have in common is a huge elemental power score. That means when they attack, their opponent's HP falls fast. Hector also boasts the cool Mana Spring skill, so he generates more mana than most – which means more special moves!

ARENA MODE

TempestGuard was once the city of one thousand arenas. A place where fighters could pit their wits (and their muscles!) against each other. Lost to the marauding forces of King Boneshaker's Skull Army, it is time to return to the city and reclaim the battle arenas, one brawl at a time.

WARRIOR RANKS

15 SQUIRE	10 SWORDMASTER	5 CONQUEROR
14 NOVICE	9 CHAMPION	4 WARLORD
13 APPRENTICE	8 GUARDIAN	3 OVERLORD
12 BRAWLER	7 HERO	2 EMPEROR
11 WARRIOR	6 VANQUISHER	1 LEGEND

ARENA LEVELS

Take your time to work your way from Squire through the ranks to Legend. The more battles you win the higher your ranking.

Careful – once you've reached the rank of Warrior, your defeats will cost you points!

Keep an eye out for the golden spear. This prized javelin is awarded to those warriors who show particular prowess on the field. Impress the crowd and amass your perfect strikes to earn your golden spear. Available for use by any of your warriors, finding your mark is not as easy as a normal strike. Throwing blind means only the most skilled will be able to defeat the enemy with a single blow – but for those who do, riches await.

BEYOND THE BATTLE

Continue your journey with World of Warriors, explore undiscovered lands, play new games and discover exclusive facts about your favourite characters.

Visit *www.worldofwarriors.com* to travel the Wildlands and continue your training to become a legendary warrior.

COMING SOON

- Discover new warriors to join your army.
- Explore the Wildlands and beyond. Discover all-new battle locations.
- Test your mettle with epic competitions.

- Fight to the end with fearsome new games.
- Become battle ready, take your campaign off-line with downloads and activities to print out, share and show your warrior skills.

UNLOCK THE SECRETS OF THE WILDLANDS

A warrior's journey is never complete,
If cruelty and darkness they seek to defeat.
Though the future is hard to see,
You must travel on to truly be free.
Come, share my vision of future toils,
So you may claim victory and share the spoils.

YOUR ARMY

Keep a note of which awesome warriors you've collected from the Temple of Epics by ticking them off here!

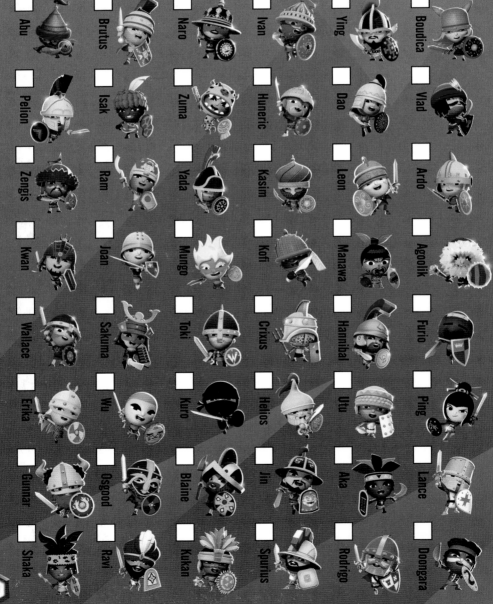

☐ Abu
☐ Brutus
☐ Naro
☐ Ivan
☐ Ying
☐ Boudica

☐ Pelion
☐ Isak
☐ Zuma
☐ Huneric
☐ Dao
☐ Vlad

☐ Zengis
☐ Ram
☐ Yada
☐ Kasim
☐ Leon
☐ Ardo

☐ Kwan
☐ Joan
☐ Mungo
☐ Kofi
☐ Manawa
☐ Agoolik

☐ Wallace
☐ Sakuma
☐ Toki
☐ Crixus
☐ Hannibal
☐ Furio

☐ Erika
☐ Wu
☐ Kuro
☐ Helios
☐ Utu
☐ Ping

☐ Gunnar
☐ Osgood
☐ Blaine
☐ Jin
☐ Aka
☐ Lance

☐ Shaka
☐ Ravi
☐ Kukan
☐ Spurius
☐ Rodrigo
☐ Doongara